Forever
and the
Night

LAURA DeHART YOUNG

Bella
BOOKS
Ferndale, Michigan
2001

Bella Books, Inc.
P.O. Box 201007
Ferndale, MI 48220

Printed in the United States of America on acid-free paper
First Edition

Editor: Lila Empson
Cover designer: Bonnie Liss (Phoenix Graphics)

ISBN 0-931513-00-7

For Dudley,
the man of my dreams

"If dogs don't go to heaven...
I want to go where they go."
—Anonymous

Chapter One

The financial figures in the Excel file were starting to blur. It was already dark outside. Without looking at her watch or glancing out the window behind her, she could feel Monday winding down. An eerie quiet had settled over the building. Even with her office door shut she could sense the absence of almost everyone.

Kay Westmore blinked at the computer screen and rubbed her eyes. She hated the endless stream of budget reports that held her hostage through the month of October. Now it was mid-November and the final figures were due to Washington next week. She grabbed her coffee cup but the contents smelled stale. Without taking a sip, she swung her chair away from the credenza until she faced the cluttered desk. In front of her, next year's budget was stacked three inches thick. Personnel forms, salary reviews, and memos from Washington fought for the remaining space. National Park visitor registries, new equipment requests for field offices, and other status reports littered the floor. She was drowning in a sea of paperwork and bureaucracy that had become commonplace over the past three years. Ever since she had been promoted from senior park ranger to regional director of the Alaska National Park Service, her work life had become the view of four walls.

Kay rested her head in her hands and squinted hard, trying to force her mind to clear. Everything was a jumble. Everything was a mess. Between her personal life and her job responsibilities, she felt like a different person from who she was several years ago. She felt out of touch with herself and the people around her.

A knock at the door snapped her to an upright position. Surprised that there was someone else in the office, she ran her fingers through her hair, grabbed a pen, and said, "Come in."

Kay glanced up, expecting to find anyone but the person she saw. The fair complexion, long auburn hair and all-knowing smile made her drop her pen. She could sense her mouth gaping, her eyes bulging with surprise.

"Kay, I'm not a ghost. I'm your boss."

"Grace, how are you? Sorry if I seemed so surprised. It's just so great to see you. It's been quite a long time since your last visit."

"Yes, far too long. I finally couldn't take another day in Washington D.C." Grace Perry, secretary of the interior, shook Kay's hand warmly. "How are you, Kay?"

"Couldn't be better." Kay helped Grace with her coat. "I was actually finishing up the new budget for next year."

"What budget?"

Kay laughed. Federal budget cuts for the National Park Service had been especially fierce over the past two years and didn't look any more promising for the next. "It can't get much worse."

Grace sat down, straightening her suit jacket and skirt over the same perfect hourglass figure Kay remembered from their last meeting. "No. Quite frankly, I think we'll at least stay level next year. I don't anticipate any further cuts. The budget is something I'd like to discuss, but that can wait until later."

"What can I help you with?"

Crossing her legs, Grace let one of her pumps dangle from her foot. "No more shoptalk right now. Tell me about you. It's been, what? Three or four months?"

Kay leaned back in her chair and smiled. Grace's tone hadn't changed — commanding yet somehow pleasant. It had been exactly three years since Grace's last visit to Fairbanks. During that visit, Grace was not yet her boss but a colleague with a joint mission to inspect the Alaskan pipeline. They had forged an uneasy working relationship that had somehow turned into an uneasy friendship. Grace was talking as a friend now, and Kay knew where the conversation was leading. But she wasn't about to give in that easily. Discussing her personal life with her boss still seemed uncomfortable. "It's been three months. Since the land management conference in D.C." Kay pointed to the phone. "You know, most of the time I can't even get you on the phone. You've become far too popular in Washington. Traveling in all the best social circles. Making quite an impression on the president, too. Or so I hear."

"Pay no attention to anything you hear. It's all sludge from the Washington sewers."

"Even the good stuff?"

Grace raised her eyebrows. "That most of all."

"So, what's he like to work for? I've only met him once for about ten minutes."

"Who?"

"The president."

"He's smart, analytical — tough and compassionate at the same time. Too bad he's married."

"That is too bad."

"We see eye-to-eye on most things. I advise him. He listens — then makes his own decisions. Of course, you always have to weigh the political factor. All the special-interest groups vying for leverage."

"Like every environmentalist group in the country."

"Yes. My in-box is full of mail from the National Audubon Society, the Sierra Club, Greenpeace USA, and the National Wildlife Federation. I've learned a lot about birds."

Kay chuckled and shook her head. "Can I get you something to drink? Coffee? Soda?"

"No. But in a few minutes you can take me to dinner. However, just for the record, you never answered my question."

"Which was?"

"How the hell are you, Kay?"

"Maybe we should save that conversation for after dinner."

"Very well. But don't you have to make a phone call before we leave?"

"Phone call?"

"To home?"

Kay cleared her throat. Stef. She would have to tell Grace about Stef, and she wasn't looking forward to it. So far she had avoided having that conversation with anyone except Russ, Alex, and Pat, all of whom were her closest friends. "No. I mean, I don't think it's necessary."

"Well, we better head to dinner then. I can see we have a lot of catching up to do."

It was the same restaurant Kay and Grace had visited three years earlier to enjoy a celebratory dinner. The Chena

4

Inn was located on the river of the same name and was a renovated old Fairbanks hotel that Kay loved. Its rooms were candlelit and intimate, and its food superb, including the best salmon in Alaska.

Grace smiled broadly as they approached the entrance — two heavy wooden doors that led to a small foyer with a stone floor and lead-glass windows. "I was hoping you'd bring me back someday. We shared a great victory here, didn't we?"

"We did," Kay agreed. "It's a day I'll always remember."

As Grace ordered her dinner and made inquiries about the wine list, a slow-motion replay of everything that had happened three years ago flashed through Kay's mind. That day in the Fairbanks conference room when she had first met Grace, before Grace became her new boss. It had started with an inspection of the Alaskan pipeline in the dead of winter, a trip that followed the pipeline through the frigid wilderness all the way from Fairbanks north to Prudhoe Bay.

But what was supposed to have been a routine pipeline inspection rapidly became mired in the political machinations of Washington. Grace was in the thick of it all, vying for her current cabinet position. Kay's boss at the time, Edward Donnelly, had also been deeply involved. So much so that he lost his job. This paved the way for Kay to take his place and for Grace to take her place among the Washington elite. Since that time, Kay had seen Grace sporadically when she traveled to Washington at Grace's bidding. Mostly they interacted by telephone and e-mail.

"What are you thinking about?"

Kay smiled and sipped her wine, a dry Chardonnay. "Actually, I was thinking about our adventure three years ago. Seems like another lifetime."

"Yes, it does."

"Don't laugh, but I miss that time. That . . . adventure."

"I know."

"You do?"

Grace flashed an all-knowing smile. "You're no bureaucrat, Kay. If it weren't for your many years of experience traveling the wilds of Alaska, I'd be dead. I haven't forgotten."

"That's kind of you to say. By the way, how's your daughter?"

"Maria's just fine." Whenever Grace spoke of her daughter, her face softened and her voice resonated with pride. "She's eleven now and quite the young lady. She started taking riding lessons this fall."

"Hey, that's a hobby you can enjoy with her."

"Kay, really. You know I can barely ride the back of a snowmobile, much less a horse."

Kay cleared her throat. "Ahem, yes. How true." Kay remembered all too well the unsuccessful snowmobile lessons necessary for their trip to inspect the pipeline three years back. Grace had overturned one too many snowmobiles and ended up riding along with Kay, her fingers digging into Kay's waist as they sped along the icy trails between Fairbanks and Prudhoe Bay.

"So now that you've asked me about my personal life and you've avoided saying anything about yours, I'll just come right out and ask. How's Stef?"

The waiter interrupted, serving the deep-fried mushrooms. Kay's mind wandered again. Stef had been her lover for three years. Kay was fifteen years older than Stef and had been hesitant to commit to the relationship from the beginning. But the sweet and loving younger woman pursued her endlessly and finally commandeered her heart. Grace knew about her relationship with Stef and had always been supportive.

"You had to ask that question, I know. It's the polite thing to do." Kay barely choked down a sip of wine. Recently, all that she once feared had come to pass.

"Kay, what's wrong?"

"She's leaving me," Kay answered in a horse whisper. "I

feel like I'm losing the best part of my life." Shaking her head, Kay blinked the tears away. She hated this — the having to tell everyone part. People thinking, "Sure, you couldn't make this relationship work either." Remembering that Grace was her boss, Kay composed herself by taking a deep breath. "This time with Stef was always fragile — at least in my mind. I don't know what I was looking for three years ago. Whatever it was, it was obviously a mistake."

Grace flinched at the news. "I'm sorry."

"The thing is, Stef's found someone else. She's in the process of moving out."

"When is she leaving?"

"Next week."

"Is she still going to live in Fairbanks?"

"Yes."

Grace fingered her wineglass. "You were both so happy."

"I thought we were."

"And Stef pursued you for months. I mean, she traveled all the way to Prudhoe Bay to tell you how much she loved you."

"Yes, she did. But I hate to say this." Kay clenched her jaw. "Age offers a different perspective on things. You know, no rose-colored glasses. You see things just the way they are because you've lived it every day. Am I making any sense?"

Grace frowned. "Vaguely."

"What I mean to say is that Stef's so young. She's got this wonderful blind enthusiasm for life I just couldn't seem to share. And I think it's from not being jaded by things like bad relationships and stressful jobs and the loss of people you love. Stef takes everything at face value because she can. And I think that's pretty cool. But it wasn't me. I have to analyze everything. I kept busting her bubbles." Kay smiled, imagining Stef at her playful best. "Bubbly. That's Stef, you know. Overflowing with life."

"Yes, I know."

"Anyway, I couldn't keep up with that. I only ended up making her unhappy. Being old and practical and sensible. Cautious and protective. *Boring*, in a word."

"I'd hardly call you boring, Kay."

"Oh, but I am."

"How do you mean that?"

"Give me a good book, a comfy chair in front of a fireplace, a glass of wine, and I'm content. Forget parties and bars and dancing. I'm all over the dyke drama stuff. Who's dating whom. It all changes from one week to the next anyway."

"You don't enjoy drama? Remind me not to invite you to Washington anytime soon."

"I told you. I'm boring."

Grace poured Kay another glass of wine. "Then you need to find someone who will share your passion for boredom."

"It's not just that. I think I took Stef for granted. It's a mistake I've made in the past. One that I obviously haven't learned from yet."

"It wasn't that way with Barb."

The mention of Barb's name made Kay shudder. Barb had been Kay's lover for five years before Stef. It was a rocky relationship that included Barb's constant verbal and emotional abuse of Kay. "Well, I think I certainly did take Barb for granted. That's why she was so much in my face all the time. I guess that's why I fell for Stef. She was so sweet and loving. And she didn't give up, you know. It was hard not to be attracted to that."

"What now?"

"My personal life is what it is, and there's not much I can do about it right now. I think I'll put relationships on hold for a while. I don't seem to be very good at them."

"And how has your work been?"

"I would like to get out from behind that desk, Grace. I'm sorry. But I'm dying, drowning in paperwork. I miss the travel, getting out into the field more. There are so many park assessments that need to be done. But for the past six months I can barely keep my head above water with the administrative side of the job."

"Good thing I decided to pay you a visit then. Tomorrow we'll spend the day reviewing the budget and planning the upcoming year. I have a few surprises for you."

"Surprises?"

"Listen, I know you've been drowning in the bullshit. I apologize for not scheduling this time with you sooner. But you've been doing a terrific job, which has given me time to concentrate on other matters. However, now we need to make some changes."

Kay squirmed in her chair. "Changes?"

"You look suddenly ill. I know it frightens you when I get personally involved in things, Kay. But trust me, all will be well."

Kay was skeptical. The fact that Grace had flown all the way to Fairbanks meant something big was brewing. Something very big. "Isn't that what you said before we went on our trek through the Alaskan wilderness three years ago?"

"Something like that."

"The same trip that almost killed us."

"The operative word there is *almost*. You and I both know that *almost* doesn't count."

Kay slid her briefcase onto the floor and hung her coat in the closet. Stef was lounging on the living room sofa, legs bent at the knee, slippered feet sticking out from underneath a knit throw. The television was blasting and Stef appeared mesmerized. Stef sipped coffee and then rubbed her eyes with a closed fist. Surveying the room and the hallway that led to the bedrooms, Kay noted that it was piled high with moving boxes.

"Hey, how's it going?"

Stef gasped and clutched her chest. "God, I didn't hear you come in. You scared me half to death."

"Sorry." Kay pretended to sort through the mail — anything to avoid those lovely green eyes. "Done packing for the evening?"

"Yeah. Taking a break. You're late."

"Had a guest arrive at the office just as I was leaving. Grace Perry. Flew in without warning."

"Really?" Stef swung around. Her blond hair was tied back, and her green eyes were as bright as a sunlit meadow. "Wow, she hasn't been around for a while."

"No, she hasn't. Not for three whole years." Kay nodded toward the television. "What're you watching?"

"Some old movie. I don't know."

Kay glanced at the screen. Immediately she recognized Shirley MacLaine. The actress was standing in a kitchen talking to Jack Lemmon. "It's *The Apartment.*"

Stef bounced to her feet, gesturing excitedly, her flannel pajamas a size too big but sexy nonetheless. "Listen, I'm moving the stuff over to the new place tomorrow. I'm sorry, Kay. I know it's a mess."

Kay laughed and crossed her arms across her chest. "I wasn't talking about this apartment. The movie you're watching. It's called, *The Apartment.*"

Stef contemplated Kay then the television. "The movie? Oh yeah. The woman's pretty screwed up, and this nerdy guy's trying to help her. He made her spaghetti and then strained it through a tennis racket. Pretty weird, huh?"

"It's a very famous scene."

"But, Kay, the movie's so old. It must have been made in nineteen thirty or something, 'cause look, it's in black-and-white." She cocked her head to one side. "I mean, like who are these people?"

Kay's shoulders slumped. "Jack Lemmon and Shirley

MacLaine. And I guess Ted Turner hasn't colorized this one yet."

"Colorized?"

"Never mind. But it's a good movie. You should finish watching it."

Stef yawned. "Nah. I'm tired. Going to bed."

"So am I. Have a feeling tomorrow's going to be a long day. Grace is here, and that can only mean something big. But that's okay. I hope it's a trip. A long trip deep into the wilderness."

Kay lay in bed and stared at the ceiling, arms tucked behind her head. Once again, her mind drifted back in time to the pipeline adventure with Grace in the Alaskan winter three years ago. All during that trip she had fought to deny her feelings for Stef. The bitter cold had helped to numb them. Her frequent run-ins with Grace and the constant challenges of the pipeline inspection also proved to be a distraction. But in the end, when she inspected those last few yards of oil pipeline at Prudhoe Bay, she had come face to face with her emotions in a raw and unexpected way.

A soft knock at the bedroom door jolted Kay from the pillow. "Yes?"

A flood of light from the hallway filled the shadowed room. "Kay, can I come in?" Stef lingered uncertainly in the doorway.

"Of course. Can't sleep?"

"My brain — it's like racing a hundred miles an hour. But I didn't want to wake you up. I didn't, did I?"

"No. Actually, I was just lying here mulling over the day's events."

Stef sat at the edge of the bed. "Is Grace really sending you away again?"

"Don't know. But if she is, quite frankly I welcome it. I'm

tired of sitting on my butt preparing reports and writing doomed budget proposals."

"Yeah, but she's probably going to send you into the wilderness again on some dangerous trip like she did three years ago. I worried myself sick while you were gone."

"I came back okay."

"Sure, after practically being buried in a blizzard."

"That was quite an experience. You know what kept me going?"

"What?"

"Thoughts of you. Of how we danced at the club that one night. You know. The first night we made love."

"When I pretended to be locked out of my dorm room."

Kay laughed. "Yes. That was such a dirty, rotten trick."

"It worked, didn't it?"

"Yes, it did. And I thought you were so sweet and innocent."

"I wanted you."

Kay closed her eyes to stop the tears. No one had ever wanted her like Stef. "I know."

Stef ran her hand across the covers. There were dark circles under her eyes. "Are you terribly angry with me, Kay?"

Kay blinked again, cleared her throat, and then lied. It would be easier that way. "No. All I really want is for you to be happy."

"I never meant for this to happen. Honest." Stef bowed her head and began to sob uncontrollably.

"Hey, hey. We've already done the crying and yelling and all the rest of that nonsense." Kay pulled Stef into her arms. "We made mistakes, and this is best for both of us. We'll still see each other. Be friends."

"Do you mean it?"

Kay meant it but didn't believe it. "Of course I mean it. I'll always love you. Nothing's ever going to change that."

Stef intertwined her fingers with Kay's. "I never cheated on you, Kay," she said, gasping between sobs.

"I never thought that. Not for a minute." Kay swallowed hard. She had uttered another lie. And she wondered if Stef hadn't uttered one too. "As soon as you met Jan you were honest about the feelings you felt for her."

"I couldn't lie to you."

"I know. I'm glad you didn't. It's made it much easier on both of us."

Stef kissed Kay's hand and curled up next to her, holding on tightly. Her sobs softened and her breathing deepened. When she was finally asleep, Kay pulled the blanket over her, stroking her hair, kissing her cheek.

Tuesday morning, Kay pulled her Toyota RAV into the office parking lot just in time to grab one of the plowed spaces. It was snowing hard. Last night she'd tossed and turned fitfully, unable to think of anything but Grace's sudden arrival and Stef. With Stef snoring lightly at her side, she'd finally given up trying to fall asleep and bolted out of bed.

For a while she paced back and forth at the end of the bed, the floorboards creaking softly beneath her bare feet. She had learned to live without sleep in the last few months. Walking the floors, wondering if Stef would come home. Wondering what she could do to change what was happening. Not much had changed. Their relationship was over, and she still paced.

Finally, Kay sat down at the bedroom window, watching the snowfall. Flakes hit the window and dissolved into droplets of water that ran together and froze outside the window sill. The night was suddenly quiet, muffled by the heavy wet snow. But nothing quieted her thoughts. This morning, her boots crunched through what the city plow had left behind. Huge uneven piles of snow bordered the end of the lot where the large yellow machines had packed new snow against old. It would be April before the piles would melt and the snow-covered parking spaces could be used again.

Russ was in the break room making coffee. The massive, burly man turned and smiled. "Morning, chief. Heard you had company last evening."

Kay shook her head. "Word travels fast."

"Yep. Rachel saw the two of you at the restaurant last night. She was leavin' with her husband. Next thing you know, she's callin' me on the phone at eight o'clock last night, yappin' a mile a minute. My ears are sore."

Rachel was the office busybody. She was also Kay's administrative assistant — a precarious combination. "Where is Rachel?"

"She's pickin' up some breakfast. Said she'd be a few minutes late. I guess she wanted to make sure our guest of honor got fed." Russ followed Kay into her office. "Why's the big boss here? Must be somethin' mucho importanto." Russ cocked an eyebrow and sipped his coffee, handing Kay a mug of her own. "That's Spanish for 'top-secret.' "

Kay chuckled and sat down. "Hell if I know. Guess I'll find out today."

"Just for the record, if Grace even mentions the word *pipeline* — even if she only gets the *pipe* part out, lemme know. I'm outta here."

Kay threw her head back and laughed hard. It felt good. Russ could always make her laugh. It was the quality about him she appreciated most, aside from the fact that he was one of the top environmental and land-management gurus in the country. "You'll be the first to know everything. As always."

Russ sat down and stroked his beard. It was deep brown peppered with gray. "I'm just bettin' it's some political thing. We're goin' on a mission of mercy again, Kay. I can feel it."

"It's obvious that Grace doesn't show up to extend her personal regards without good reason. She certainly hasn't bothered to do so in the last three years. And she did tell me yesterday that, and I quote, 'I have a few surprises for you.' That was after I told her that my butt was getting sore from sitting at this desk all day."

14

"Hey, boss. Please don't encourage her, okay?"

"Russ, don't give me that crap. You're up for an adventure as much as I am."

"Okay, maybe a little overnight trip to one of the parks might be fun. Say, you look kinda beat. You okay?"

"Didn't sleep too well."

"Stef?"

Kay swallowed hard. "I thought it would get easier."

"Look, Kay, I've got some idea of what you've been through these last few months. Every day I've seen that look on your face. Now that Stef's actually movin', it must be harder than petrified caribou shit."

"It is. Like a kick in the stomach."

"Petrified caribou shit? Mr. Bend, you have such a way with words."

Russ stood up, turned, and bumped right into Grace, who was standing in the doorway. "Uh, Grace. Hey, it's so great to see you."

Grace smiled warmly and removed her brown leather gloves. "A pleasure to see you as well. Please have lunch with Kay and me today. Twelve-thirty sharp."

"I'd love to. Lookin' forward to it. See you later." Russ stepped aside and let Grace pass. Then he hurried out the door.

"Kay, good morning." Grace sat down and opened her briefcase. "Certainly could be better without this dreadful snow. It's such a nuisance. I've never been able to tolerate the stuff since our unpleasant excursion a few years back. Must have been that horrid ice pit we were buried in."

"That wasn't much fun, I agree," Kay said, more than slightly amused. "But it does snow in Alaska. Happens quite a bit, actually."

Grace plopped several file folders on the edge of Kay's desk. "Aren't you perky this morning? Good, we can get right down to business."

"Secretary Perry?" a voice said from the doorway. "Excuse

me for interrupting. You probably don't remember me, but I'm Rachel Stewart, Kay's assistant. We talk on the phone quite a bit."

"Rachel, why of course. How are you?"

"Good, thank you. I've made some coffee for you." Rachel was juggling two coffee mugs in one hand and a large tray of pastries in the other. "I see you already have some, Kay. Do you need a refill?"

"No thanks. I'm fine for now."

"Okay, I'll just leave this tray of goodies, too. I picked them up on my way to work. Fresh from the bakery at the end of the street." Rachel set the tray of pastries on the small conference table. "So nice to see you, Secretary Perry. Will you be in town long?"

"Good to see you, Rachel. Just for a day or two." Grace accepted the coffee, then swung back around and shot Kay a look of impatience.

"Thanks again, Rachel. Can you please shut the door on your way out?"

"Oh, of course. If you need anything else just let me know."

The door shut softly and Kay grinned. "Sorry about that. She means well."

"Hmm, yes. I'll have to be careful how I use the word *perky* around here. Compared to her, you're quite sedate." Grace tasted the coffee. "Makes good coffee though. Now where were we?" Grace was wearing a striking gray suit with a pink silk shell, a single strand of pearls, and pearl earrings. She crossed her long, shapely legs and sat back in the chair, tapping her fingers lightly on the arm. "Oh yes. Barrow, Alaska. That was what I was about to say. Ring a bell?"

"Yes, of course. I've only been there once. Quite a few years ago." Kay's mind began to process information. Barrow was a city of thirty-five hundred Alaskans resting at the northernmost tip of the state and was accessible only by air. Some Alaskans referred to Barrow as the "top of the world."

Located along the shores of the Arctic Ocean, it was a city inhabited mostly by the Inuit Eskimos — or "The Real People," as they preferred to be called. For two months out of the year, Barrow lay in darkness with temperatures dipping to minus fifty-six without the wind chill. Kay cleared her throat. "What about Barrow?"

"One moment. Let's skip to something else." Grace pointed to the file folders she had laid on Kay's desk. "The National Petroleum Reserve. I'm sure you're familiar with that stretch of land."

"Certainly." Kay thumbed through the file folders and inwardly cringed. The National Petroleum Reserve had been a political war zone for the last three years. This stretch of land, comprising almost five million acres, was originally set aside for gas and oil leasing. After the Exxon *Valdez* accident in 1989, environmentalists put enormous pressure on Washington to close that area of land to any further leasing. It was only recently, after years of environmental hearings and political lobbying, that the northeast quadrant of the reserve was finally opened to leasing bids.

"You're deep in thought, Kay."

"Yes, well, the reserve's been a political hot potato as you certainly know."

"Firsthand. I finally got enough political support and clout to open up the northeast quadrant — after pacifying every environmentalist organization in the state, mind you. Promised to leave five hundred and eighty thousand acres untouched. Gave in to almost every demand and concession you could possibly imagine. And now the problem."

"The problem?"

"Yes. The Eskimos are already crying foul, claiming that the oil companies are violating the leases by entering some of the protected areas. Seems that during the molting season geese heavily use the shallow lakes north and east of Teshekpuk Lake. There are some caribou migration issues as well. You can read the report for yourself. It's all there." Grace sipped her coffee and pursed her lips. "A series of meetings will be held in Barrow at the end of the first week in January. Environmentalists, Eskimo representatives, some of my staff, and you."

"Me?"

"I need you to help mediate and to assist in the investigation of these alleged violations. We've invested heavily in the lobbying efforts to reopen the leasing of this land. Again, we're talking national security. The government needs more natural gas and oil resources developed. Any violations by the oil companies and we'll have serious problems that may lead to the revocation of the leases." Grace shook her head and said firmly, "I do not want to lose these leases. I want a handpicked government team there first to carefully survey the situation and find out what's going on before a hoard of environmentalists and reporters descend on the area and cause untold PR problems."

"I understand."

"There will be several inspection teams deployed. You'll head the team that will handle work in the Teshekpuk Lake region. Obviously, it's the most critical area of concern."

"What are we looking for?"

"Contaminated lake water from chemical or petroleum runoffs. Work areas constructed in the restricted zones. Deployment of any equipment or drilling in unauthorized locations."

"I get the picture."

"I've established some key contacts for you in Barrow to help you with your investigation. We need to strike a balance here, Kay. To protect these sensitive environmental areas, at the same time allowing the oil companies to conduct their work. It's not going to be easy. You're not likely to run into many friends on either side."

"Sounds like fun."

"I try to save the best ones for you, Kay. Sorry. But we're talking millions of dollars here. In energy reserves and in

18

years at the legislative tables. A setback now would be devastating." Grace shrugged. "Wouldn't help my political career much either."

At precisely twelve-thirty, Russ drove Kay and Grace to lunch at the Marriott Marquis in downtown Fairbanks. Sitting at a white linen–covered table near the front window overlooking the street, Kay watched a group of tourists as they boarded a bus. Tourism in Alaska thrived all year long. Most of the tourists were bound for some fishing expedition or survivalist camping trip, Kay guessed. Their duffel bags and backpacks, in every neon color imaginable, were stacked in a high mound near the bus's luggage compartment.

Grace recapped the upcoming trip for Russ's benefit. "I want you to accompany Kay. You're a great team. You proved that once before. Whatever equipment you need, whatever accommodations — it's not a problem."

"When are the first meetings being held?" Russ asked, cutting into a thick steak.

"The end of the first week in January," Grace answered.

"Nice way to begin the New Year." Russ shifted uncomfortably in his chair, wiping his hands on the cloth napkin draped across his lap. "Who's gonna be at these meetings?"

Grace donned a pair of reading glasses and flipped through a few pages of a typed report. "The government by way of you and Kay. An Alyeska Consortium representative. Don't have a name yet. Representatives from some state environmentalist groups. The board of the Inupiat Northern Council. Also a legal representative I've personally chosen from the Bureau of Land Management. Her name is Lela Newlin and she knows the issues surrounding the reserve area very well. Lifelong resident of Alaska. More importantly, she's a full-blooded Inupiat."

Kay wasn't surprised. Inupiat were Eskimos of the northern arctic. The Inupiat had lobbied fiercely against granting new leases, particularly in the Teshekpuk Lake area.

19

Choosing Lela Newlin as a panel member was a shrewd political move on Grace's part. "You seem to have every angle covered, Grace. As usual."

"As I explained earlier, these meetings and this investigation are crucial." Grace slipped off her glasses and sighed heavily. "And I certainly hope this is the last crisis during my cabinet tenure. I've had my share, and I'd like to leave some positive legacy. Maybe increased energy reserves will be it."

"At what expense?" Kay asked boldly.

"None, Miss Westmore. It's the balance that we strike and that's always been my message. That we cherish and preserve the land. Yet, at the same time, use the natural resources that are available to maintain our energy security."

"That philosophy may qualify as an oxymoron," Kay asserted.

"You're getting irritable in your old age, Kay. You've definitely been cooped up in the office too long."

"Cooped up? Yes, that's true. But not entirely out of touch." Kay pushed her plate away. "At any rate, thank you for allowing me to take Russ. I'll need him for the trips into the reserve. Equipment, supplies. Heading trouble off at the pass. Those are Russ's specialties."

"I'm very much aware of Russ's capabilities. And I wouldn't have you make this trip without him."

Russ finished his Coke. "I wouldn't have her make the trip without me, either. The oil company crews won't welcome our presence, and there could be trouble. If not trouble, then difficult weather and travel conditions, especially in the reserve. There's nothin' near Teshekpuk Lake but some small Eskimo villages. The rest is raw wilderness."

"Yes, you'll need to be extremely careful. These adventures don't seem to happen at the most opportune time of year, do they?" Grace commented. "But I can't take the credit this time. You can thank the environmentalists and the Inupiat Northern Council for scheduling these January meetings.

Quite frankly, I prefer Washington to a trip to Barrow in January. And that's saying a lot."

"It's going to be dark there," Kay said, almost to herself.

"Dark?" Grace asked.

"Yes. In Barrow the sun sets in late December and doesn't rise again until the first few days in February."

"Good grief, I'd forgotten." Grace frowned and dangled her eyeglasses between her fingers. "And no one at the office bothered to remind me of that incredibly important detail. No one at all."

Kay looked at Russ, then back at Grace. "Be sure to tell them back in Washington that they're sending us on a trip in the darkness and bitter cold smack-dab in the middle of the Alaskan wilderness. I hope whatever we're looking for we can find in the pitch blackness."

Grace pounded the table with her fist. "Oh, this is absolutely ridiculous. How in the world can you be expected to conduct this kind of work in the dark?"

"There are ways, Grace. Russ will think of something, won't you, Russ?"

"Heck yeah. First, we better order some big old flashlights," Russ said, scribbling a note on his legal tablet. "Three weeks of January night in beautiful Barrow. No sun at all. It's gonna seem like forever. Someday I'm movin' to Florida, I swear."

Kay nodded in agreement. "I'll be living right next door to you."

Chapter Two

Kay's father was asleep in front of a blaring television. It was still half an hour before lunch, so she sat in the chair next to him and allowed him to nap. Last week, they had celebrated Thanksgiving together. Kay had taken him to one of his favorite restaurants downtown for a traditional holiday meal. It had been a good day for her father, a day when his illness gave him a brief reprieve.

For almost three years Kay's father had lived with her and Stef. Kay bought the home for all of them. Her father enjoyed his own separate living area downstairs in the large, split-level house. But during the last year his health had begun to deteriorate rapidly. Parkinson's disease had ravaged his mobility, and even experimental brain surgery had failed to stop the advance of the disease. Since the surgery, his mental health had also begun to fail. He hallucinated, forgot to dress himself, was disoriented.

Finally, Kay sold the house to raise the extra money she needed to place her father in an assisted-living facility. She had no choice. He needed specialized daily care. For months she researched the facilities in Fairbanks and surrounding communities. She didn't want her father to end up in the kind of dump her sister had put him in years before.

When it was time to move, her father never gave her an argument, exhibiting a quiet understanding that the change in living arrangements was necessary. He actually liked his small, private apartment. The daily professional care had slightly improved his health, she thought. He was around other people and enjoyed the singers, musicians, and other activities planned weekly by the facility. On good days he even played bingo.

Kay gently shook her father's shoulder. He woke with a start and stared at her, his head cocked sideways.

"Kay. Is it lunchtime already?"

Kay leaned closer to her father. He spoke in a whispered slur, and she could barely understand him. "Yes, Pop. Do you know what's on the menu today?"

"No."

"What do you say? Let's go find out."

Sliding the blanket from her father's legs, Kay discovered that he was dressed only in a shirt and underwear. "Pop, where are your pants?"

"Over there."

Kay grabbed a pair of navy Dockers lying at the foot of the bed. "Okay, these will do for lunch."

"I can't put them on."

"It's okay. I'll help you."

"They have to be washed," her father said haltingly.

"Hmm, they look clean enough to me. But I'll get another pair anyway." She rummaged through his dresser but couldn't find any slacks. "Where are all your trousers, Pop?"

"Under the bed."

Kneeling on the floor, Kay peered under the bed. She counted five crumpled pairs. "What are they doing down here?"

"Can't wear them."

Totally confused, Kay eyeballed her father suspiciously. "Are they all dirty?"

"They need to be washed because of the bugs."

"Bugs?"

"Bugs. All over the place." Kay's father snatched a flashlight from the table next to his lounge chair. Clicking it on, he directed its beam at the rug in front of him. "See. Bugs. Everywhere."

Kay peered at the floor. She saw nothing. "There are bugs on your pants, too?"

"And in my orange juice."

Kay's face tightened with worry. Obviously, her father was having more hallucinations caused by the powerful drugs that had been prescribed to control his Parkinson's. Last week it had been snakes. "What if I take this pair and shake off all the bugs?" Kay held up the navy pants. "Then you can put them on."

"Okay."

Her father watched intently as Kay shook the pants, laid them on the bed and wiped them off with her hands. "There. That's better. Now let's get you dressed."

Lunch was a salad for Kay but a smorgasbord for her father. Eating was still his greatest joy, though no one would ever guess it from his small frame. Kay poked at her salad while her father waded through a large fruit cup, turkey casserole, green beans, baked apples, Jell-O, and cookies for dessert. Much of the food ended up in his lap or on the floor but he continued eating, undeterred. While her father attacked his plate with a spoon, Kay talked about her job and the new adventure Grace had just announced. Her father listened intently, grunting at the appropriate moments.

"I don't think this will be anything like that trip I was involved in three years ago, so I'm not too worried. I'm just happy to be getting out of the office."

"Will you be gone a long time?"

"Well, the good news is that I'm not leaving until after the holidays. Then I think I'll only be gone about six weeks."

"Oh. Is Russ going?"

"Yes, he is."

"I like him. He's smart."

"We take good care of each other. So please don't worry about me."

"I always worry."

"Daddy, here you are. I went by your room but couldn't find you."

Closing her eyes for a brief moment, Kay prayed for strength. It was her younger sister, Julia. Her stomach immediately began to churn. "Hello, Julia."

"Kay, so nice to see you." Julia plopped down next to their father and kissed him on the cheek. "Just came by to check on Daddy."

Kay sipped her soda and forced a smile. "It's been awhile. How are you?"

"I'm great," Julia said, twirling her bleached blond hair with her forefinger. "How are you, Daddy?"

"I'm done eating. Tired. Take me back to my room, Kay," her father instructed, struggling up from his chair. Shakily, he gripped the table, his back toward Julia.

"Sure, Pop. Let's go."

Humming a Madonna tune, Julia sauntered a few steps behind them all the way back to their father's room. After saying good-bye to her father, Kay turned around to find Julia gone. She peeked around the corner and spied Julia waiting for her at the end of the hall. She was tapping her foot impatiently, fingers still entwined in her hair. It was an annoying habit she'd had since childhood.

"Why do you always have to be such a bitch, Kay?" she asked sulkily. "How long are you going to hold a grudge anyway?"

Kay folded her arms across her chest. Four years ago there had been an ugly competency hearing filed by Julia against their father. Believing firmly that her father was still able to handle his own affairs, Kay contested the hearing. Julia and her husband, Jack, subjected both Kay and her father to a lengthy court hearing that was vicious and painful. In the end, Kay's lifestyle was used against her, and Julia and Jack won guardianship. "Julia, I have not been a bitch. I was trying to be nice, for God's sake."

"You barely said hello to me," her sister said with a sniff. "You're still holding that grudge."

Kay gave up her fight for composure. "First of all, I did say hello to you. Second, what grudge could you possibly be talking about, Julia? The fact that you spent all of Pop's money and pawned him off on that dump of a nursing home like he was a piece of trash four years ago? Or the fact that you broadcast my personal life all over Fairbanks and in the courts?"

Julia held out her hands and stared at her bright red fingernails. "That was a long time ago, Kay. Ancient history." She waved her hands as if bored with the conversation.

"Not ancient history enough. You're always harping on it."

"It's your attitude, Kay. I can tell what you're thinking. You know this all could have been put behind us. But what do you go and do? Poke your nose into everything, take Daddy out of the nursing home — and now he's right back in one anyway."

"This is a helluva lot better place than the trash heap you incarcerated him in. He actually likes it here."

Julia pursed her lips and rolled her eyes. Her hip-hugging

26

jeans and snug red turtleneck flattered her size-eight frame. "This place must be costing you a pretty penny."

"We're managing, thank you very much. Now, if you don't mind, I've got things to do."

"Hmm, well I know you're not running off to see your girlfriend. I hear she dumped you for someone else."

Kay could feel her ears turning as red as Julia's sweater. "That's none of your business."

Julia's eyebrows fluttered. "It's true then."

"Yes, it's true. And I'm sure that makes you very happy."

"It doesn't make me happy, Kay. I just wonder why you can't find a normal relationship that lasts for more than a few years."

"I guess I'm unlucky in love," Kay answered sarcastically.

"Maybe." Julia unwrapped a piece of gum and started chomping away. "I personally think it's a lesbian issue. There's no such thing as a life partner. First sign of trouble and gays give up. No commitment."

"Since when have you become an expert on the gay lifestyle?"

"Since you've been my sister."

"I don't need your two cents, and I'm certainly not interested in your observations concerning my personal life." Kay stalked away, grinding her teeth until she got to her car. She could feel a headache coming on, the same headache she always got after being in her sister's presence.

Ducking under the balloons and streamers, Kay found a corner in the living room and squeezed into it. Sipping her beer, she had a good view of the television and the New Year's countdown being broadcast from New York City. Thousands of people were making merry, jammed like sardines into Times Square in the bitter cold. In Fairbanks, midnight was still hours away, but everyone wanted to see the celebration in the city where the famous ball dropped and mobs of people partied well into the morning. If it was midnight in New York, it might as well be midnight all over the world.

Kay checked out the room and felt like a sardine herself. Her best friend, Alex Chambers, and her partner of ten years, Pat Kinsey, were throwing the party. Alex and Pat's house was chock-full of people, mostly women, intent on ringing in the New Year with as much hoopla as possible.

"Kay, try one of these." It was Alex balancing a large tray of homemade hors d'oeuvres over her head. "They're cheese filled. Yummy."

Kay stood on her tiptoes and snatched one of the tiny pastries before a crowd descended on Alex. Sliding the tray onto the coffee table, Alex squeezed into the same corner occupied by Kay.

"Hey, doll. What do you think of my pastry?"

"Al, there's no one who cooks like you. No one."

"Now I know why we're best friends. You say all the right things."

"And mean them, too."

Alex kissed Kay's cheek. "I'm glad you're here. Why don't you join me in the kitchen? It's the one room that's off-limits to everyone else."

"And they say the best parties happen in the kitchen."

"Not in my house. C'mon. We can talk. It seems like ages."

"I don't want to monopolize the hostess's time."

"The hostess is ready for a break. The guests can fend for themselves right now."

Compared to the rest of the house, the kitchen was downright serene. Kay slumped into a chair while Alex stacked some dishes in the sink. "Where's Pat?" Kay asked, tossing a Goldfish cracker into her mouth.

Alex threw a dishtowel over her shoulder and leaned against the counter. "Downstairs in the den playing Nintendo Sixty-Four."

Kay chuckled. She often referred to Alex and Pat as the odd couple. Alex was a gourmet cook, loved to read, and had a passion for classical music. Pat loved eating at McDonald's, was a pinball and electronic game fanatic, and wasn't happy unless Melissa Etheridge was blaring at full volume. "You two amaze me. You're so different and still so happy. I think it's great."

"After ten years, you begin to appreciate the differences and celebrate them as challenges. But it's not always easy."

"I don't think it's meant to be."

"How did Stef's move go? Are you okay? You haven't talked about it much."

"Stef's good. And I'm fine."

"I wish I believed that, babe."

"Okay, so I don't lie very well. I still think about her every day."

"Maybe your trip will be a distraction."

"It comes at a great time."

"Speaking of your trip, why is it that Miss Perry always sends you away at the most God-awful times of the year? Making you fly to Barrow in January. Ridiculous."

"Can't blame Grace. The Inupiat Northern Council and a bunch of environmentalist groups kind of forced the issue with the Bureau of Land Management. So the meetings were scheduled right away."

"Doesn't the bureau fall under Grace's authority?"

"Yes, but she's trying to keep her distance from this one. She doesn't want it to look like she's interfering. At least not yet."

"So she's sending you and Russ to play politics for her. How nice."

"As far as I'm concerned, anything's better than sitting at that desk all day. And, as you said, I welcome the distraction right now."

"It's almost midnight in New York. Wanna go watch the ball drop?"

29

"Hey, why not? It's not like we've never seen it before. But it is tradition."

Alex grabbed Kay's hand and pulled her out of the chair. "Happy New Year, Eastern Standard Time, Kay. I love you."

"I love you, too."

Alex kissed Kay lightly on the lips. "I'm sorry you've been unhappy. I hope this year will change that for you."

"Listen, don't rush me into any new love affairs, Al. I think I'll remain chaste for a while if you don't mind."

"Chaste! That'll be the day, Westmore. Look, you're even stealing a hug from my girl." Pat strode into the room and grabbed them both by the arm. "Get out here, the ball's about to drop. Then we get to celebrate all over again in a few hours."

Alex draped her arm around Pat's shoulder. "Don't worry, darling. I saved a special kiss just for you when midnight really arrives."

The ball dropped in Times Square, and the New York crowd went wild. A few hours later, the local crowd went wild and multicolored confetti flew around the room in every direction. The party guests cheered, kissed, hugged, and tooted those annoying horns. In between enthusiastic hugs from well-meaning friends, Kay tried to feel some joy for the coming year. What would be different, she thought — except that she would be alone? Stef would not be there in the morning to kiss her awake, to greet her in the kitchen with day-old jelly doughnuts and too-strong coffee. There would be no midmorning phone calls or passionate lovemaking at lunch. In the evening the apartment would be empty — waiting for her like it was now with its hollow echoes. There would be no giggling laughter or playful wrestling on the sofa. And no Chinese takeout in front of bad rental movies that almost always turned into a ten o'clock tryst.

Kay's eyes suddenly stung and she felt nauseous. All along she had told herself that things would be okay. That life

30

without Stef would be okay. For a while, she had managed to fool everyone, including herself.

"Kay! Kay! We're going to make a toast."

Kay accepted a flute of champagne from Pat and forced a smile. "A toast. Of course."

"Happy New Year!" Pat raised her glass. "Good health, plenty of money, and awesome sex in the coming year to everyone!"

Kay sipped her champagne and thought, Well, two out of three ain't bad.

Two days after the New Year, Kay and Russ barricaded themselves in her office for the entire lunch hour, planning the upcoming trip to Barrow. Maps and papers were scattered everywhere. Russ was munching on his fourth piece of double-cheese pizza while reviewing a map of the National Petroleum Reserve. "We're gonna need snowmobiles. I'm gonna have a dozen shipped up to Anakruak. We'll need to use the winter trails to get to Teshekpuk Lake."

"Winter trails? I assume we're talking about frozen waterways and land."

"Yep. Actually, it's easier travelin' around that area at this time of year with everything frozen over. Believe it or not, this same trip during the summer would be a pain in the butt."

"You mean the Inupiat Northern Council and the government did us a favor by sending us in the dead of winter?"

"Yeah, can you believe it?"

"Not hardly."

"Anakruak will be a good base of operations. There's not much there but a small Eskimo village. But at least there's shelter and supplies available." Russ traced his finger along the winding winter trail that began at Anakruak and wound dangerously through the ice and snow to the north and east of Teshekpuk Lake. "The winter trails end on the eastern side of the lake. When we travel south, we'll be on our own."

Kay rubbed her temples. "This is going to be interesting. South of the lake there's nothing but frozen wilderness for hundreds of miles."

"Nope. A few tractor trails. But that's it. I've planned our supplies down to the last waterproof matchstick. No room for error here. If the weather turns bad or our equipment fails, we'll be stuck in the middle of nowhere."

"What about the equipment we'll need to document any violations by the oil companies?"

"I'll have everything we're gonna need waitin' for us at Anakruak. Surveying equipment and video cameras to make sure that the oil companies are working where they're supposed to be. Camera equipment, water-testing kits, food, and other survival supplies just in case they're needed. Plus, the team from the EPA will be bringing some of their own supplies."

"As usual, you've got all the bases covered."

"I hope so. Listen, have we figured out what this trip is really all about? Is this some Department of the Interior politico cover-our-butto movement that Grace has started? I mean, she is the one who pushed to have these leases granted."

"If we find a lot of infractions, it's not going to look good for Grace. That's a fact."

"There's always cover-up mode. Find out what's gone wrong and clean it up before it's official front-page news."

"That would be my guess. Regardless of what proof or information the Northern Council or environmentalists have, the government can always counter with its own lily-white report. Behind the scenes Grace can gnash her teeth at the oil companies and threaten their asses."

"I think we have this one figured out already, boss."

"After the last trip three years ago, we're a little bit older and wiser."

"Ain't that the truth. Listen, I'm gonna be about a week behind you. I want to fly to Anakruak first and make sure everything we need gets there and is ready when we are. I'm gonna fly up to Barrow on Tuesday after the meetings are over, if that's okay with you."

"That's fine. By that time I'll know more of what we're up against. That is, if I can cut through all the politics and other bull that'll be flying fast and furious at the meetings."

"See, that's what I like about us, Kay. We work so well together. You take on the politics, I take on the logistics."

"I should make you attend the meetings out of spite. I doubt if I'll be seeing any friendly faces there. I'll miss yours."

"You'll be fine. You can handle that stuff. I'd be bustin' up the place and tellin' everybody where to go."

"Remind me how you ended up working for the government in the first place."

"I promised them I'd stay hidden in the wilderness."

Kay gathered up the maps, reports, and file folders. "I think I promised that too. At least until Grace came along."

"Grace thinks a lot of you. And so do I."

"Thanks. I'll keep that in mind. It may be the only thing that keeps me going for the next six weeks."

Later that evening, even though she was exhausted, Kay forced herself to go jogging. The upcoming trip would be enough of a physical challenge. But for the past few days, she had been restless. The jog would help to clear her mind. Halfheartedly, she finished tying her sneakers and was just about to leave the apartment when she heard a knock at the front door. Opening it, she was shocked to see Stef bundled up in a heavy sweater and bright red ski vest.

"Hi ya, Kay. Knew you were going away Monday, and I wanted to stop by and say good luck. Hope that's okay."

"Sure. C'mon in."

"You look like you're on your way out."

"Was just going for a jog."

"It's snowing."

"Is it?"

"Not real bad or anything. It's one of those wet snows with the huge flakes."

"Oh. Well, that won't stop me from running. I've jogged in worse than that."

"I know. You're crazy." Stef laughed quietly and crossed her arms. "Crazy in a nice way."

Kay felt awkward, uncomfortable. As much as she enjoyed seeing Stef, she wished she'd left ten minutes earlier. "At least you qualified that. How's everything at the new place? You all settled in?"

"Not quite. I have boxes stacked up to the ceiling in the den. Mostly books and clothing."

"It'll take awhile to sort through things. I hate moving."

"It sucks. I feel like totally disorganized."

"I haven't done a thing with this place since you left. So I guess that makes two of us."

Stef bit her lower lip. "Listen, Kay, please be careful on this trip. I'll worry. The last time Grace planned a trip for you, you almost died in a storm and your coworker got shot."

"No need to worry. Russ'll be helping me out. We'll be fine."

"Russ is going with you?"

"Yes."

"Good. He looks after you. I feel better already."

"My father said the same thing. I don't think you people trust me to take care of myself."

"We do. It's just that it's so dangerous and all. Especially at this time of year."

"Listen, you have a new life now. You don't need to worry about me anymore."

"That hurts, Kay."

"I wasn't trying to be hurtful. But these feelings of protectiveness and not completely letting go are all going to pass, Stef."

"I thought we were going to be friends. Friends worry about each other."

"Yes, they do." Kay was suddenly annoyed and struggled not to show it. Then she was hurt and struggled not to show that. It was hard standing there talking to Stef without reaching out for her, without taking her into her arms. "Look, you're building a whole new life for yourself. You'll do new and exciting things with Jan, meet different people, make new friends. Maybe even learn to ski."

Stef finally smiled. "You were supposed to teach me to ski."

"I tried. You were awful."

"Yeah, I was pretty awful. It's a good thing you gave up on me. I might've killed somebody."

"The thought had crossed my mind."

A single tear fell onto Stef's cheek. "We had some fun, didn't we Kay?"

"We did."

Stef caught the tear with her glove. "I'll call you when you get back. You still want me to, don't you?"

"You can call anytime."

Stef gave Kay a quick hug and then disappeared down the steps. For a few moments, Kay was frozen in her tracks, unable to think or move. Minutes later, she was jogging down her street, the large flakes of snow stinging her face. Her legs felt disconnected from the rest of her body, her feet dropping like lead weights along the snow-covered path that followed the banks of the Chena River. There was a burning in her chest and she gasped for air. Her throat ached and her vision was blurred. Changing direction, she veered off the path toward a tall pine tree along the road. She braced her hand against the tree to steady herself, struggling for a deep breath. She thought about Stef and the first time she had put her arms around her, dancing in that smoky bar three and a half years ago.

The young woman's curves fit into Kay's as though the two of them had been parted at birth. The warmth was not unwelcome. Kay's travels from one side of the state to the other left little time for romance.

Stef's head rested on Kay's shoulder. Her hair was fragrant and baby soft. But she was a baby. What am I doing, Kay thought?

Stef wrapped her arms securely around Kay's neck. Looking directly into Kay's eyes, she asked, "Where were you, darling?"

The word *darling* threw Kay off balance. "Pardon?"

"You said you just got back from a trip."

"Gates of the Arctic. National preserve up north. Ever been there?"

"No. Will you take me?"

Kay laughed. "Maybe."

"I'd keep you warm."

"No doubt."

"Being a forest ranger, you must know all the nifty spots. Romantic. Private."

"A few. Still at the university?"

"Yep. Full-time now. My education grant finally happened, so I cut back my hours at the alumni office to part-time. With the grant, and a little help from Daddy, I'm in pretty good shape."

Kay ran her hands along Stef's sides, stopping at her hips. "Yes, you certainly are."

Stef giggled softly, flicking Kay's right earlobe with her tongue. "Thank you."

Stepping back, Kay tried to compose herself. "Well, we better sit down and finish our beers. Can't make this a late night. Important meeting tomorrow."

Stef grabbed Kay's arms. "This is an important meeting too, Kay. I know we've met before, but this time's special. I can feel it."

She grasped Kay's hands and leaned upward, her soft mouth finding Kay's, gently biting Kay's lower lip.

Kay drifted away — from the music, the room, the hour. She was locked on Stef's lips, sensuously parting her own, on the tongue that slipped inside her mouth. No. This couldn't be happening now. This mustn't happen now.

The memory faded and the tears came. Resting her forehead against the cold bark of the tree, Kay listened to the heavy sobs as though they belonged to someone else. And they did. They belonged to the Kay who had been deeply in love and had lost that love many years too soon. She beat the tree with her gloved fists until they hurt. Why? Why did she ever let Stef into her life when she knew that it would never work? The snow continued to fall and Kay continued to stand underneath that stupid tree. Numb from the cold, she finally started back home. She had done enough running for one day.

Chapter Three

Kay peered out the plane window and scanned the shadowy white landforms below. It was just past noon on Monday, but only blackness met the shimmering snow at the horizon, drawing a faint line into the January night that would last for another four weeks. The twinkling lights of Barrow, a city located three hundred miles above the Arctic Circle, were the only sign of life in this northern most wilderness.

Twenty minutes later, Kay was scurrying off the tarmac into the small airport terminal. Russ would be following in a week with a helicopter and the other supplies they would need for trips into the National Petroleum Reserve. Kay's first task was to meet with Lela Newlin of the Bureau of Land Management. Lela was to be Kay's main contact and liaison for the balance of the trip.

Kay had done her homework. During the course of her research, she discovered that Lela Newlin was an extremely capable government attorney and spokesperson for the Bureau of Land Management and, most important, a respected voice in the various Inupiat communities located throughout northern Alaska. Newlin was also influential with many of the state's most outspoken environmentalists. Even though she worked for the federal government, Newlin had managed to cut through a heavy layer of distrust by communicating, fairly and impartially, the environmental concerns of the northern Alaskan communities.

Duffel bag hoisted over her shoulder, Kay strolled into the terminal area. She had arranged to meet Newlin at a small café near the terminal's front entrance. With one quick scan of the immediate area, Kay spotted the shop. The café consisted of a small counter and about five tables and chairs. It was the only coffee shop, and only one person was seated inside — a small-statured woman with coal-black hair and a deep bronze complexion. She was sipping coffee and reading a newspaper.

"Excuse me," Kay said, dropping her duffel bag onto the floor. "Miss Newlin?"

"Kay Westmore?" Lela offered an outstretched hand. Her gray-black eyes were striking as they searched Kay's. They were an unusual color, reminding Kay of smoke wisps from a farmhouse chimney on a crisp autumn day. "So pleased to meet you. I trust you had a good trip."

"Yes, it was just fine. Thanks."

"Please, Miss Westmore. Sit. I will get you something. Coffee?"

"Great. Cream only."

"Cream only," Newlin repeated as she stepped away to the counter.

Kay threw her jacket over the chair. She watched Newlin

as she ordered two coffees. Her long straight hair flowed to the middle of her back. She was about five-foot-two or -three at most, Kay thought. Her physique was unimposing but solid, her movements self-assured. Her native skin color was a tawny bronze, the color of a sunlit horizon at dusk.

Conscious that she was staring, Kay picked up the newspaper and glanced at the front page. The National Petroleum Reserve had made the headlines already. The meetings between federal government representatives, environmentalists, and the Inupiat Northern Council were being well publicized for later that week.

"You see, we have made the local news today," the steady voice said in a precise, even tone. "And not a word from the meetings has been recorded yet."

Kay glanced up and smiled. "This Friday's going to be an eventful day for everyone involved, I'm sure."

"Yes. But all will be well."

"I like your confidence."

"We must always hope for the best. You look tired from your long trip, Miss Westmore. I will take you to your hotel now."

"Thanks. And please call me Kay."

"Of course. And I am Lela." Lela got up, her granite eyes reflecting the brightness of the overhead lights. Her full lips broke into a pleasant smile. "Your hotel is downtown. It is some miles from here. Perhaps an hour's drive."

"I appreciate the ride."

"It is not a problem."

The snow crunched beneath the truck's chain-covered tires. Along with the frigid air, the clinking and clanking of the tire chains kept Kay wide awake. Winding along miles of

40

frozen landscape, the two-lane road from the airport cut its way through shadowy hills and barren fields. The truck's headlights illuminated a frozen path of ice. It was no road, really, just packed snow and scattered cinders that had long ago lost their effectiveness. The air was so cold Kay thought the metal truck might snap into pieces along the stark roadway.

While they drove, Kay found herself staring at Lela. Her long dark hair was striking against the soft features of her face. Occasionally, she threw her hair over her shoulder where it bounced and lay in soft waves between her shoulder blades. With her hair back, Kay had a better view of Lela's face, oval-shaped with tawny skin that was as smooth and clear as the night sky. "Do you live near downtown?" Kay asked, trying to make small talk.

The eyes, now like cloud storms in the darkness, found Kay's. "I live west of the city. Not far from the Chukchi Sea."

"Ah, you live on the beach then."

"Yes. A frozen beach." Lela laughed. It was a musical laugh, friendly and infectious. "I do not think most people would enjoy it."

"A far cry from New Jersey or Florida."

"But no less beautiful."

"I've never seen the Chukchi."

"Then you must. I will take you tomorrow."

"That would be great. Thanks."

"I have never been to New Jersey and their . . . boardwalk?"

Kay chuckled. "Yes. The famous boardwalk."

"What is it like?"

"You eat food that's not good for you, play silly games, go on rides that make you dizzy, and sit on benches and watch the ocean. And the people."

"Have you done this? It sounds like fun."

"I have relatives in the Northeast. I used to go to the Jersey shore in the summer during college. Get a summer job and a nice tan."

"You are blond and so fair. I cannot imagine you with a tan."

"Yeah, well, I was young then. Now I use sunscreen or I burn."

"I would not need to go to New Jersey for a tan," Lela said with a broad smile.

"No, just for the boardwalk experience," Kay agreed, laughing.

Lela had made reservations for Kay at a hotel called Top of the World. It was just south of the Chukchi.

"Here you will not be far from the frozen sea, Kay. So close you can walk there."

"For once I get to be a tourist on one of my trips. Usually I'm the guide."

"You have never been to Barrow?"

"Many years ago, but only for a few days. It was for a government meeting, and I didn't get to see a thing except the inside of a downtown hotel."

"Then I will happily be your guide. Except for attending college and graduate school, Barrow has been my home since I can remember. It will be my pleasure to share it with you."

Tuesday morning, Kay slid out of bed, rubbed her eyes, and staggered toward the windows. She pulled the drapes open and stared into the morning blackness. Her internal body clock was already a mess. Even at eight in the morning it was completely dark outside. The street and traffic lights flickered against a clear, black sky.

She was looking forward to the day. Actually, she was looking forward to spending the day with Lela. Something about Lela intrigued Kay. She wanted to learn more about her and the life she lived here in Barrow.

At around nine-thirty, Lela picked her up in front of the hotel. She was dressed in a heavy green nylon parka, jeans, and boots.

"Good morning, Kay. Did you sleep well?"

"I passed out last night as soon as my head hit the pillow."

"Did you have something for breakfast?"

"Yes, thanks."

"Good. I will be your tour guide today. Since the meetings do not start until Friday, I will show you Barrow and the beautiful Arctic."

"Sounds great."

"At lunch we can talk about our plans for the meetings. Some strategy is probably wise."

"You think we're going to run into much trouble?"

"There will be many delicate issues discussed. It is hard to say what will happen."

"I appreciate any insight you can give me."

"My pleasure." Lela glanced up at Kay and said, "You are tall."

"Excuse me?"

"You seem taller today. Or I am getting even shorter."

Kay looked down at her feet. "I've got my serious cold-weather boots on today. I wasn't sure where we'd be going."

Lela smiled warmly. "That was a diplomatic reply. You did not say, Lela, you are short."

Standing on her tiptoes, Kay said, "You know, now that you mention it, you are pretty darned short."

Lela chuckled softly. "I like the diplomat in you much better."

~ ~ ~ ~ ~

43

Lela drove through town, heading north to the coast. The terrain was treeless, the coastline icebound. Even in the darkness the vast whiteness of space that was the sea was clearly visible. Mountains of ice jutted into the sky — icebergs many stories high that once cruised swiftly through the seas, now trapped until the summer thaw. They were mammoth sculptures frozen in time, strangely beautiful against an eerie black sky.

"It always amazes me how people can live and flourish here," Kay said, staring out of the truck. "I mean, it's incredibly beautiful. But what kind of life can you really make?"

"Here my people have lived for two thousand years," Lela said, her eyes searching the horizon. "We are the Inupiat, a tribe of the Inuit," she said proudly. She made a sweeping motion with her arms. "We began by moving back and forth along the coast or up and down river valleys with the changing seasons. Survival was our biggest challenge. It required all our energy and ingenuity to survive."

"And now?"

"Now there are satellite dishes and cabins, prefab houses, snowmobiles, and VCRs. But still the challenges of the land are here. They have not gone away completely." Lela tugged her gloves off and fumbled for the knobs on the dash. She cranked up the truck's heat and pulled the parka hood over her head. "What has changed this land the most — the way my people live — is the government. And the oil."

"How so?"

"Until the oil and the pipeline came to be in the early seventies, most of my people lived a life of subsistence. Then the state became rich overnight. Suddenly, there were NANA Corporation dividends, Alaska permanent fund shares, welfare, and food stamps. The Caucasian workers came to take the oil jobs. Eighty percent of our villages remained unemployed. In Barrow, unemployment is still very high. But our purpose in life was never to drill the land. To live off of it, yes. It has gotten harder and harder to do this. There are more people, tourists, pollution. And for some it is hard to live beyond the outstretched arm of the government."

Kay was stunned by Lela's words. "Are you blaming the government?" she asked sharply. "I mean, it seems a bit hypocritical. You work for the government."

Lela shook her head. "No, I do not blame the government, Kay. Change comes. Sometimes it is good, sometimes bad. I thought I could best serve my people by teaching them what is good about the government. They already know what is bad."

Lela's reply struck a chord with Kay. It had been honest and deeply felt. "I'm sorry. I didn't mean to get defensive. I have this constant battle going on inside myself, too. What I think the government does right and what I think it does wrong."

Lela smiled and touched Kay's arm. "No need to be sorry. Let me show you where the caribou cross. It is a peaceful place."

Lela drove the truck northeast along the coast. About ten minutes later, she turned south. The land was still flat, but evergreen trees now dotted the landscape to the east and west. In between the winter forests, the windswept snow formed small dunes and ripples giving some form to the open country. Overhead, the sky flashed orange, green, blue, and lavender.

"The northern lights," Kay said out loud, watching the colorful display.

Twenty minutes later, south of Barrow, Lela stopped the truck alongside the icy roadway. "The sky is clear. January is not the best time to see the lights. But the weather is ideal this morning."

The lights were still exploding across the heavens. Kay gazed at the continual flashes erupting against a cloudless sky. It was nature's own gigantic light show. "I know it has to do with particles from the sun being thrown against the earth, but that seems too scientific for something so beautiful."

"Yes, it does. I prefer to think of the lights as something more spiritual. It is the land talking to us with help from the sky." Lela pointed to the vast, white tundra in front of them. "Here, in the summer and early fall, under these same flashing heavens, the caribou herds cross. A half million of them. They return always to the calving grounds where they were born."

"I've heard that. Pretty amazing."

"This will be an issue on Friday, Kay. My people claim that some of the crossings off-limits to the oil companies are being disturbed. Particularly in the Teshekpuk Lake area."

"What do you think?"

"I know only what I hear. It may be fear speaking. I cannot be sure. What I do know is that there is an ancient bond between the caribou and my people. The caribou are to the Inupiat what the buffalo were to the American Indian. They mean survival. Food, clothing, a sense of pride, and ritual of the ancient days all come from the caribou hunt. It is a spiritual time, those summer days."

Kay listened to Lela's impassioned words and studied the dark tundra, trying to picture a half million spindly-legged creatures with enormous antlers and bulging eyes navigating that vast space. "If the caribou crossings are being jeopardized, we'll find out."

"The land sings whatever you wish to hear. That is what the Inupiat say. When we visit the reserve, the land there will tell us what we need to know."

Lunch was in a small native restaurant outside of town. The building reminded Kay of an old fishing shack that had been enlarged. Inside, simple wooden tables and chairs were spread throughout the main room. The only other room was in the back of the establishment where a variety of aromas filtered into the dining area. The handwritten menu was an eyeopener, and Kay chose the whitefish, which seemed fairly safe compared to some of the other menu items: polar bear, walrus, and caribou. Kay also chose a beer to wash the food down just in case.

"You are not being brave, Kay. The walrus is quite good. It is often coated in herbs and spices and deep-fried."

"I eat mostly fish anyway. And lots of vegetables."

"Then you should have tried the grayling. It is not always on the menu."

"I've heard of it. What's it like?"

"It is much like salmon. Do you eat salmon?"

"Yes, it's my favorite."

"Then I must bring you again and you will try the grayling."

"It's a deal."

"Are you a good cook?"

"Who, me? My God, no. Most of what I eat comes out of a box and goes into a microwave. Unless I have friends over. Then I make one of them cook."

Lela laughed until she was holding her sides. "Then I must make dinner for you, Kay. It seems to be a rule among your friends."

"Anybody who cooks for me is a friend for life."

"Then we will be good friends. I never cook out of a box."

"You have my sincere admiration." Kay sipped her beer and found herself once again drawn into Lela's eyes. They communicated a simple honesty and openness that made her deeply attractive.

"Is there something wrong, Kay?"

Realizing she was staring again, Kay snatched a paper napkin and opened it on her lap. "No, there's nothing wrong. I was just thinking about Friday. How do you really think the meeting will go?"

"I have heard some rumblings already. The meeting may be contentious. My people are fearful of the land leases granted to the oil companies. And the environmentalists will also be there. They will use their leverage too. There are some

47

powerful environmental lobbies in Washington, as I am sure you know."

"Yes, Grace Perry and I were discussing that fact the last time we met."

"Sometimes the environmentalists use my people to further their own agendas, I am afraid. They use fear to incite the Northern Slope villages. Some of the facts they present are true, but many times exaggerated. When you combine these exaggerated truths with my people's own experiences, there is often panic."

"What have your people's experiences been?"

"With the government, mostly good. Some bad. Broken promises that are not forgotten. Experiences with the oil companies and their workers, mostly bad. The oil companies do not respect the land or the native peoples. There have been many cases of violence, thievery, and destruction in our villages. Many times the government does nothing."

"How have you addressed these issues?"

"With much patience and education. I try to teach my people how the government works, good and bad. I have told them that this time things will be different. That the government will force the oil companies to respect the land."

That was another passion Kay shared with Lela — a fierce protectiveness of the land. "If there are any infractions, that's what we intend to do. Force them into compliance."

"Then we will hope for the best on Friday. And we will also hope that the oil companies send no representative. It will go much easier on us if they do not."

"Grace said there would be a representative from the Alyeska Consortium there. But during our briefing she didn't have any details."

"Let us hope they send someone who can maintain a calm atmosphere."

"An associate of mine will be joining us next week. Russell Bend. He's coordinating the members of the EPA teams that will be assisting us on our expeditions into the National

Petroleum Reserve. He's also in charge of all the equipment we'll need."

"It sounds like we will be well prepared for our investigation."

"Russ takes care of every last detail."

"And you?"

"I allow Russ to take care of every last detail so that I can do the work that I love. The land is everything to me, too."

"Then my people will like you. They will feel your honesty and commitment."

Kay was touched by Lela's words. "And you?"

"You are strong like my husband was. I can feel that in your spirit. My people will feel that too."

Chapter Four

As far as Kay was concerned, Friday morning arrived much too soon. The meeting room in the local chamber office was large yet stuffy. Two tables with microphones had been placed in the front of the room facing many rows of folding chairs. Kay paced and watched the people file in. Though there were some women and Caucasians, the audience was comprised almost entirely of men, most of them Inupiat and many of them members of the Northern Council.

Lela was sitting at one of the front tables studying a map of the National Petroleum Reserve. Like almost everyone else in the room, she was wearing casual attire. It was the first time Kay had seen Lela completely unbundled from her thick hooded parka and heavy sweatshirts. Dressed in a navy wool sweater over a gray flannel shirt, jeans, and boots, Lela was finally revealed in all the soft curves Kay had imagined. Nervously, Kay glanced at her watch. Ten more minutes and the fun would begin.

"Miss Westmore?"

Kay stared into the face of a man who definitely stood apart from the rest of the crowd. He appeared to be in his early thirties and was dressed in a gray suit and maroon tie. Blond hair cut short and precisely trimmed, the stranger was completely out of place in this room full of caribou skins and nylon parkas.

"Yes? Can I help you? I don't believe we've met."

"Stone Allen. Vice president of public relations for the Alyeska Consortium. Pleasure meeting you."

Kay was shocked. This nearly prepubescent man was representing the oil company interests? He puffed his chest and shoved his hands into his pockets. Taking an immediate dislike to him, Kay crossed her arms in front of her. "Kay Westmore, director of the National Park Service, Alaska."

"Yes, Westmore. I've heard all about you." His dark brown eyes bored into her.

"Really?" Not liking Allen's tone, Kay took a step back. She could feel the clench of her own jaw as she studied the smug expression staring back at her.

"I'm familiar with your reputation and your politics."

"Politics?"

"Your views are rather slanted, aren't they? Toward the environmentalists. Against the oil company concerns," he said in an accusatory tone.

A throbbing began at Kay's temples. "Listen Mr., uh, what did you say your name was?" she asked, suddenly flustered.

"Allen. But you can call me Stone."

"Allen, yes. Listen, I work for the United States government. My job is to protect the lands set aside by the government as parks and preserves. *Protect* being the operative word. Now, obviously that makes me sensitive to environmental interests. However, politics has nothing to do with it."

Allen cracked an annoying smile. "Yes, of course. Whatever you say."

Turning away, Kay stooped and whispered to Lela, "Have you met this jerk yet?"

Lela frowned. "Yes. He is on the panel."

"Terrific. We might as well go home." Kay scanned the room again. "Room's full. I think we should get started."

Lela nodded and got up. "I agree."

Kay settled into her chair, more than willing to allow Lela to moderate the discussion. Stone Allen sat next to her. Also seated at the table were representatives from two key environmental groups based in Alaska. Kay had met them each briefly while the room was being setup for the meeting. Though they appeared to be levelheaded individuals, they expressed strong concerns about the petroleum reserve and the leasing grants given to the oil companies.

It was a full house, standing room only. To open the meeting, Lela spoke a few words in Inupiaq and then switched to English. She welcomed everyone and reviewed the agenda and the issues to be discussed. First on the agenda was the representative from the Alaska Wilderness League, John Singleton, who lived in Singiluk, northeast of the National Petroleum Reserve.

Singleton talked first about the reserve and the government's promise to let this land go undeveloped, particularly after the Exxon *Valdez* disaster in 1989. "Now the government's changed its tune and has granted leasing privileges to the oil companies. And within three months of that contract, there are already documented violations."

At this statement, the crowd in the room began to murmur and come alive. A buzz of whispered conversation put Kay on edge.

Singleton continued. "What kinds of violations? Heavy

equipment moving through the restricted zones. Garbage and chemicals dumped near Teshekpuk Lake. Drilling and excavation near the caribou crossings."

The phrase "drilling and excavation near the caribou crossings" caused the room to erupt with angry comments and gestures. Lela stood up and spoke in Inupiaq, attempting to restore some calm. Singleton interrupted her and continued for another ten minutes in what became a ranting discourse on the evil oil companies and on the government that had betrayed them all. Kay felt a trickle of sweat at the nape of her neck. Things were going as badly as she feared.

"The bottom line is that the National Petroleum Reserve is the largest expanse of untouched wilderness left in the United States. It's home to one of the world's largest caribou herds, arctic wolves and foxes, grizzlies, moose, eagles, whales, polar bears, and millions of migratory birds." Singleton pointed a finger at Stone Allen of the Alyeska Consortium. "Can we trust *him* and the other oil companies to honor the restrictions and limits placed on the leases recently granted by the government? Can we? Based on the evidence we already have, I think we have our answer."

Singleton's ally, Mark Townes of the Alaska Center for the Environment, was next to speak. He reiterated much of what Singleton said and added a few more incendiary remarks, effectively disrupting the meeting for a full ten minutes. In between disruptions, Lela spoke calmly to the crowd in Inupiaq. But her words had little effect. Finally, Stone Allen got up to address the group. The mere mention of the name of the oil consortium, Alyeska, caused individuals in the room to mutter some strong epithets not quite under their breaths. Though most of the utterances were made in Inupiaq, it didn't take a genius to figure out that what was being said was not complimentary.

Allen held up his hands. "Please give me an opportunity to speak. The oil companies have worked very hard since nineteen-eighty-nine to rebuild their trust with Alaskan residents. It certainly would not be in our best interests to allow violations of the leasing agreements to take place in the National Petroleum Reserve," he continued undaunted. "It would not serve the oil company's interests to violate the lease agreements. And it certainly would not honor the trust placed in us by the people of Alaska or the representatives from the United States government sitting here at this table."

Someone booed loudly from the back of the room. Another person yelled for Allen to sit down and shut up.

"Please let me finish," Allen pleaded. "The new leasing agreements in the reserve carefully balance the impact on a fragile Arctic landscape and its abundant wildlife with the long-term economic future of Alaskans."

"Economic future? If there are no caribou, we will have no economic future!" a voice yelled.

Allen shot back, "Then the next time you receive your Alaska Permanent Fund Shares or NANA Corporation Dividend checks, tear them up!"

Kay cringed and jumped up. The crowd reacted similarly, jumping from their seats, yelling and shouting. Someone threw a pen that sailed like a missile over Allen's head. "That was a very stupid remark," she said in Allen's ear. "What were you thinking?"

"I hate these people," Allen hissed, slipping out of the room through a side exit that led to the building's administrative offices.

"What do you want me to do?" Lela asked matter-of-factly.

Kay studied the angry mob. It was clear nothing else would be accomplished that day. "Tell them we'll resume Monday at ten o'clock. Tell them the United States government has a few things to say about all this."

Lela spoke in Inupiaq, trying to yell over the noise. She finally shouted something at the top of her lungs. Kay was impressed that such a thunderous, commanding tone could emanate from this tiny woman. Immediately, everyone was silent. Lela then spoke to them for a few minutes in a calm, quiet tone. After she finished, they all left in silence.

"What in the world did you say to them?" Kay asked.

"I told them that their elder spirits would be ashamed of them. And that the spirit of the land would not be still until they heard all sides."

"Is that it?"

"That — and a few other choice words," Lela said, a mischievous gleam in her eyes. "I scolded them like children and shamed them into silence, I am afraid."

"Good job. I'm keeping you close at hand on Monday when I finally get my say."

"I'll be sure to stay close at hand."

"Please do." A look passed between them, and Kay felt a strange twinge in the pit of her stomach. She ignored it and boxed the rest of her papers, maps, and file folders.

Kay left the chamber hall in search of Allen. She found him using someone's desk phone and, with her finger, cut off the connection.

"Do you mind? I was on a business call."

"Tough. We need to talk."

"Listen, what happened in there has been brewing for months. It was inevitable."

"I don't believe that. I also don't believe that a public relations professional could say something so idiotic. You certainly didn't do the oil companies any favors. Of all the unbelievable things to say."

"I'm tired of coddling these people. And so are the oil companies, quite frankly. We've been kissing their collective butts for years. Exxon has paid millions in damages and clean-up fees and are no further ahead than they were in nineteen-eighty-nine. I've had it. The oil companies aren't violating any restrictions in the reserve, and I intend to prove it. Maybe then we can move on and get back to the business we do best — providing energy to the people of this country."

"Nice speech, Allen. But on Monday when we resume I don't want to hear a word out of you. Do we have an understanding?"

"I have nothing else to say to those people."

Lela shuffled around her kitchen preparing dinner. After the stressful morning and early afternoon spent at the Barrow Chamber of Commerce, she insisted on feeding Kay. Lela's white frame house was located in north Barrow not far from the Chukchi Sea she loved. It was a modest home for an attorney and government employee, but that said a lot about Lela. In the few short days they had spent together, Kay had learned that this cheerful, intelligent, and serene woman led a relatively simple life.

"Do you have any family in the area?" Kay asked, munching on some cheese and sipping a glass of Chardonnay.

Lela covered the pot of rice she was cooking. "I have a brother who lives in Nome with his family. I see them a few times a year."

"No one in Barrow?"

"My parents have passed on. I was married many years ago, but my husband died in a hunting accident. I was in my early thirties then and had no children. So I decided to do what I had always really wanted to do."

"What was that?"

"Go to college." Lela wiped her hands on a dishtowel and sat down. "The Inupiat culture views women very traditionally. As wives, mothers, and caregivers. The woman is the spiritual center of the home. Her life is her husband and her children."

"So going to college is uncommon."

"Yes, very. Though that has changed a lot in the past ten years, I am happy to say. But it was a desire I always had. When I was young, for an Inupiat girl to go to college was

56

unthinkable. When I found myself alone after my husband died, everything became clear to me. I decided that I could best help my people by pursuing a degree and a career."

"That's extremely admirable."

"It was hard at first. There was distrust among my friends and the people who knew me. They said that I was becoming *naluaqmiut*."

"Which means . . ."

"White person."

Kay raised her eyebrows. "Oh. Not a good thing, I guess."

"That Inupiaq word is much like the English word . . ." Lela stopped, looking uncomfortable.

"The *N* word?"

"Yes. I am sorry. I did not want to say that word. Here in Barrow there is still much prejudice between the native and Caucasian peoples. It is a sad reality."

"I only know what I've read."

"When I was a little girl there were whites-only restaurants and stores. They are gone now, but the racial problems still exist."

"I'm afraid that's true in a lot of places."

"It is. And still we must all live on the land of the same spirit." Lela bounced up from her chair and slid some rolls into the oven. "Tell me about you, Kay. About your home and family."

"My mom passed away a few years ago. I've got a sister, Julia. But we don't get along real well."

"Why not?"

"It's a long story. My dad lives in Fairbanks. He's got a lot of health problems, but he's hanging in." Kay switched gears. She didn't want to talk about her family. "Anyway, I do love the Fairbanks area. Actually, I love all of Alaska. That's why it concerns me when we open up leasing rights in protected areas."

"You remind me of my husband. Robert loved the land too. And he was also afraid that the protected areas would be allowed to dwindle." Lela uncorked the wine bottle, refilling Kay's glass. "You are not married, Kay?"

A sip of wine went down the wrong way, and Kay coughed. So much for switching gears from her personal life. "No, no. Never been married."

Lela patted Kay lightly on the back. "Are you all right?"

"Yes, fine." Kay could feel her face redden. "Good wine," she said, laughing and coughing at the same time.

"You are a fine person, Kay. Why is there no one special in your life? Do you work too much?"

"Uh, sometimes. I mean, there have been people in my life. I guess I just haven't met the right person."

"I am sorry. Are my questions too personal?"

"No, no. My mind is on my work right now. That's all." Kay watched Lela as she returned to the kitchen, stooping down to open the oven. She was wearing black jeans that revealed luscious curves from hip to thigh. Her light blue denim shirt was tucked in, outlining enough above the waist to show additional curves that caused Kay to take another sip of wine.

"It is rare that I have a chance to talk with anyone. About life, I mean. I go to court for the government, make arguments, and write legal briefs about government and state land issues. Sometimes I talk with a few people I know. But they are distant. They do not understand me."

"Maybe *you* work too much."

Lela smiled broadly. "Touché. It is true. Since Robert died, my work is what I know."

"Something sure smells good."

"The fish is pike. I hope you like it as much as the wine." Lela smiled, her smoky eyes sparkling in the firelight.

"Oh yes." Kay picked up her empty wineglass. "That was my second glass, wasn't it?"

"No matter. It was a stressful day, and there is always more wine."

"Want me to get some more wood for the fire?"

"Thank you. That would be helpful."

Kay searched for her parka. "Where'd I put my coat?" she asked out loud.

"Oh, Kay, I hung it up for you. Here, put this on. It is made from caribou hide. Very warm."

"If it's yours, it won't fit."

"Actually, it was my husband's. I have kept it this past seven years as I keep his spirit in my heart. I made it stitch by stitch from a caribou he killed for meat a month before he died." Lela slipped the coat over her shoulders. "It was a birthday present. He never got a chance to wear it."

Kay was amazed that the coat fit her so well. She rubbed her hand along the soft sleeve, imagining the care and love that had gone into the making of the garment. "I'm sorry."

Lela patted Kay on the shoulders. "It was a long time ago. It's cold out there. Hurry back."

Kay grabbed the handmade log carrier and walked out into the eternal darkness. The wind whipped against her as she struggled toward the woodpile on the side of the house. Laying out the piece of canvas, she began to pile some logs on top of it. Through the side window she could see Lela moving around the small kitchen. A trail of smoke billowed from the chimney into the cold evening air. There was something peaceful about this tiny house in the Alaskan wilderness. Or maybe it was the woman inside who evoked that peacefulness. Whatever it was, Kay was grateful to be there. For the first time in a long time, she felt an inner serenity. She intended to hang on to that feeling for as long as she could.

The weekend passed peacefully. Lela had been the perfect tour guide, escorting Kay around the city of Barrow. During their excursions, Kay had learned a lot about the Inupiat way of life. They had visited a museum full of native artifacts and a history of Lela's people. Absorbing as much as she could, Kay had reached the conclusion that the Inupiat were a peaceful and spiritual people who lived from the land. It was only when the land was threatened that they became hostile, because to them the land was everything. It was life itself.

When it came to learning about the Inupiat and their way of life, the most revealing words came from Lela herself. Kay listened for hours as Lela talked about her life and the struggle of her people to survive an unforgiving wilderness.

"When I was a little girl, hunger was not a strange companion. Even the best hunters like my father struggled to put food on the table every day."

Kay passed the fruit to Lela. "That must have been scary."

"Not really. We always knew there would be more food." Lela sprinkled the fruit on to her cereal. "The women worked to find food too, you know. We fished. Hunting was done by the men."

"I thought the women did mostly domestic kinds of stuff."

Lela answered with apparent pride. "Not at all. Fishing was important. I was maybe eleven or twelve, and all the women and young girls would get into the aluminum boats to check the gill nets we'd set the day before. When we saw the floats twitching and bobbing, we knew the fish were there."

"What kind of fish?"

"Mostly small pike, whitefish, grayling. We'd have gloves on our hands, but our fingers would be numb from the cold of untangling the fish from the nets and tossing them into washtubs. The fish was dried in strips, boiled in chunks, fermented or frozen. Sometimes we ate them raw."

Kay shook her head in disbelief. Her mother and father had indulged her as a child, and hers had clearly been a life of relative ease compared to Lela's. "You're a much better woman than I am."

"Not really. I've had a different life. That is the only thing.

But you see all of this made us one people. The struggle for food. The community of sharing both hunger and plenty."

"My mom cooked for us every night. She got the food at a place called a supermarket."

"That is your culture. My people shop at small trading stores. Some now go to the local supermarket. Many still hunt and fish as we have for centuries."

Kay looked at Lela with admiration. "The heritage of your ancestry is precious to you."

"Do you not feel that with your people?"

"I'm not sure we have that obvious common thread of struggle to unite us. Maybe if we'd take the time to look back in history a couple of hundred years, we'd find it. But there's a lot that divides us today."

"What divides you?"

Kay added some cream to her coffee. "Prejudices, I think. North versus South. Black versus white. Gay versus straight." Kay studied Lela's face. She saw nothing but understanding.

"I can tell you are a woman of strong beliefs and convictions. Again, you remind me of my husband. He was strong and independent like you. Maybe even a little stubborn." Lela smiled and sipped her coffee. "Am I right?"

"Me? Stubborn? Well, yes. I think that's probably a big fault. That, and the fact that I don't seem to handle being hurt very well. I need to learn how to be more forgiving."

"Some hurts are hard to forgive."

"Maybe. Unless you've had a hand in them too."

Once again, on Monday morning, the Chamber of Commerce hall was filled with the collective voices of the Inupiat. Kay fidgeted at the head table, hoping that this meeting would end on a positive note. The same individuals were seated at the tables with her: Lela, the environmentalists, Singleton and Townes, and Stone Allen from the Alyeska Consortium. Allen had simply nodded to her when she arrived that morning. She had simply nodded back.

Lela again made the panel introductions, but this time Kay would speak first — and last, she hoped. Everyone else had stated his or her case, and now it was the government's turn. Lela turned the floor over to Kay.

Kay began by talking about the history of the National Petroleum Reserve. She mentioned the Exxon *Valdez* incident but tried not to dwell on its negative implications. Then she spoke about the new exploration leases granted to the oil companies. She emphasized the many restrictions placed on the oil companies, particularly concerning the 580,000 acres near Teshekpuk Lake, which excluded development.

A middle-aged Inupiat woman stood and asked politely for an opportunity to say a few words. Kay nodded and smiled, indicating that the woman should speak. Her voice was strong and clear, and she spoke in precise English.

"I have traveled here from the North Slope on behalf of my people to tell you that we need our lands to continue to exist as a people. But to do this we rely on the fish and caribou for food and clothing. It is also more than this. It is our culture. We understand the oil — it is part of our lives now. It is money and it is jobs for the Caucasians. It does not mean so much to us, but we have learned to understand it. We have learned that we can live both ways, having the oil but having our way of life, too. We need the government's help to continue to do this. Please make sure our caribou herds, fish, and other wildlife are safe. If they die, we die. Thank you."

Kay smiled politely. She looked at the older woman and thought about Lela fishing in the freezing cold at the age of twelve, helping to feed a hungry family. This woman had done the same, as had generations of native Alaskans before her. Fighting to control her emotions, Kay smiled again and thanked the woman for volunteering to speak. "The restrictions on leasing are clear and will be enforced," Kay stated firmly in response. "And since there have been reported infractions of these leasing agreements, a full and complete investigation will be conducted by the United States government over the next few weeks."

"How do we know you'll tell the truth, *naluaqmiut*?"

Kay flinched. The word stung because she knew it was meant to. "A member of your own community, Lela Newlin, will help lead the investigation. It will be her report, not mine, that will be presented to you here in February."

The room erupted into conversation. Kay continued, "If we find any infractions at all, the consequences for the oil companies will be severe. Financial penalties, lease revocation, or both."

"Who gives you the authority to threaten that?" Allen demanded angrily.

"The United States Government. That's who."

Laughter could be heard from the crowded room. Kay glanced out over the sea of smiles and realized who the enemy really was. Not the government, not the environmental groups, but the oil companies. It was their public relations nightmare in 1989 and it still was.

"I just want to close by saying that the leasing was meant to have nothing but beneficial consequences for everyone involved: the oil companies, the state of Alaska, the United States Government, and the Alaskan people. The intent of development is to protect the land while providing additional sources of domestic oil, increased revenues to the state and federal governments and up to four thousand new jobs. There's a great deal at stake for all of us here. Regardless, I do promise you a complete and unbiased report. Chamber officials will announce when the next meeting will be held. Thank you."

Kay got up, signaling the end of the session. The audience filed out quietly, and Kay felt an enormous sense of relief. The uproar had been kept to a minimum, and for that she was grateful. But she also knew that the next meeting would be the most crucial one of all. Whatever evidence they collected at the reserve, good or bad, would have to be presented thoroughly and convincingly to the citizens of Alaska, as well as to the environmental representatives.

"Good job," Lela said, gathering up their papers. "By the way, thank you for putting my head on the chopping block."

Kay smiled meekly. "Sorry about that. But you've got a rapport with the Northern Council. Whatever happens, the truth will be told, and they'll hear it from you. And that's the way it should be."

"Truth? Is that what you plan to give them?" Allen asked snidely. "Or just the sliced and diced reputations of the oil companies on a silver platter?"

"Just the truth, Allen. That'll be enough," Kay said calmly. "Besides, I can't slice and dice your reputation any worse than you already have."

"I hope you don't mind if I tag along while you go on this wild-goose chase for the truth. I plan to make sure oil company interests are fairly represented."

Kay shook her head. "That'll be the day I escort you around the Alaskan frontier. No way."

"Oh, but you will. In fact, I already have the blessing of your boss. You remember her — our esteemed secretary of the interior. And I will be going with you, Miss Westmore. Most assuredly, I will."

Allen stalked off, and Kay stood frozen in her tracks. "This can't be," she said in disbelief.

Lela handed Kay her briefcase. "I think this is where the politics comes to light, Kay. I believe we had begun to forget about that aspect of our assignment."

"I intend to call Grace right away. I can't believe she told that lunkhead he can go with us. What was she thinking? And why didn't she consult with me first? I could have told her what a slimy, no-good, oil-company snake he was." Kay muttered to herself all the way back to Lela's truck.

"Kay, your stubborn streak is showing," Lela said,

64

teasingly. She opened the truck door for Kay. "And I sensed such a gentleness about your spirit when we first met."

Kay threw her briefcase onto the backseat. "I used to be a nice person. I don't know what happened."

Lela climbed into the driver's side. "You have worked for the government too long, Kay. I think it has had an effect on your temperament."

"Yes, maybe that's it. Lord knows the politics of the job is enough to kill you."

Starting up the truck, Lela turned toward Kay. "You will stay at my house for the rest of your trip," she said matter-of-factly. "I have an extra room, and it is not a problem."

"Oh no. I couldn't impose like that. Absolutely not."

"You would not be imposing. It is a selfish thing I do." Lela's dark eyes searched Kay's. The tone of her voice was even softer than usual. "I like the company. It is something I have missed all these years. To be alone is sometimes good. But it can also be . . . too solitary." Fixing her eyes on the road, Lela drove the truck in the direction of the hotel. "Unless you prefer the hotel, of course."

"Prefer the hotel? Heck no. I've seen enough of hotels to last me a lifetime. You can only watch so much television in one evening."

"Then we will pick up your things and you can have a place to call home for the next few weeks."

"I hope Russ will speak to me after this. He'll be here tomorrow, and hotels are not on the top of his list either. He'll be green with envy."

"Will that cause a problem?"

"Not at all. Russ is a great guy. He'll give me some grief just because he loves to harass me."

It took about fifteen minutes for Kay to reach Grace at the interior office. Grace rarely ever answered her phone and usually had to be paged. Once Grace did get to the phone, she sounded harried.

"Yes, Kay. What can I help you with?"

"The meetings didn't go well. Not Friday's and not today's."

"Not surprising."

"My real concern is Stone Allen. He's representing the oil companies in all of this. He says he spoke to you and received your blessing to accompany Lela, Russ, and me on the trip into the reserve."

"Yes, I spoke with him. And, yes, I bestowed my blessing upon him. Is this a problem?"

For once, Kay didn't hold back. "Yes, it is. Quite frankly, he's a pompous incompetent. He nearly caused a riot at the first meeting. In the field, I think his presence will only detain and inconvenience us."

"Maybe. But his presence also gives us leverage to use down the road. If any questions are raised by the oil companies regarding compliance issues, we can say that they were fairly represented."

"I'm not sure I'd use the word *fairly*."

"Listen, Kay. This is your assignment, and I doubt very much that you're going to allow Mr. Allen to get in the way. Not with what we have at stake."

"Why is he really coming with us, Grace?"

"I don't know what you mean."

"The best result we can hope for is that we'll find no compliance infractions by the oil companies. Is Mr. Allen coming along to ensure that result?"

"Miss Westmore, minutes are precious on my end, and I don't have time to answer your improper and almost insulting questions," Grace answered sharply. "What I do know is that Allen requested to go along so that the oil company interests were fairly represented. I concurred. I think that's all you need to know."

"Yes, you're right."

"Keep me updated."

"Certainly."

The phone clicked dead, and Kay raged with anger. If all parties were to be fairly represented, why not invite representatives from each of the environmental groups, the Inupiat community, local reporters and community officials? Why not invite every citizen of Alaska? The trip was going to be dangerous enough without an inexperienced bureaucrat tagging along. Suddenly, Kay started to laugh out loud. She thought about the trip three years ago with Grace, the ultimate Washington bureaucrat. Once again, history was repeating itself. If I can survive escorting Grace Perry deep into the wilds of Alaska, I can survive anything. Let Allen come along. Whatever we find, we're going to find anyway, whether he's there or not.

When Kay peeked through Lela's living room curtains Tuesday morning, it was snowing lightly. The sky was a black-gray color that promised a day of bad weather. When Kay and Lela arrived at the restaurant around noon, Russ was already there. Sitting in an oak booth, he was drinking coffee and reading the morning newspaper.

"Hey, Russ. How was your trip?" Kay asked, hanging her coat on a brass hook.

"Ladies! Good morning." Russ folded his newspaper and got up. "You must be Lela Newlin."

Lela's small hand disappeared as Russ shook it. "Yes. Mr. Bend, it is a pleasure to finally meet you. Kay has told me a lot about you."

"Uh-oh. That can't be good. Now you know all my faults." Lela slid in beside Kay. "Actually, Kay speaks well of you."

"That's good to know. How did the meetings go?"

"Not well," Kay sighed. "And the fun's just beginning."

"Listen, the fun *is* just beginning. But we'll be prepared

for whatever we're gonna be facin' in the reserve." Russ hailed the waiter and they listened to the lunch specials. As they perused their menus, Russ filled them in on the upcoming trip. "I've got everything set up for us at Anakruak. All the equipment and supplies are there. Lela, have you seen the route Kay and I mapped out?"

"Yes, I have. You have chosen the best way, especially at this time of year. I would not make any changes."

Russ smiled and fumbled for a small black notebook in his shirt pocket. "I've checked and double-checked all the supplies. Hey, would you mind lookin' this list over, Lela? Let me know if you think I've missed anything. You can beep me later if you have any additions."

Lela clipped the sheets into a file folder. "Yes, I will review it later this evening."

"That's it then, I think. We should be ready to go on Friday. The EPA team is scheduled to meet us in Anakruak bright and early Saturday morning." Russ held out his arms. "Anything else?"

The waiter interrupted them and they ordered their lunches. Kay dreaded telling Russ the latest news. "Uh, there is one other small matter," Kay said hesitantly after the waiter left. "You may have to revise your supply list. We're going to have another guest tagging along with us."

Russ stopped mid-gulp of his coffee. "Oh my God. Don't even tell me. Grace Perry."

Lela chuckled and Kay smirked. "Uh, no. Not Grace. Someone worse, if that's possible."

"Who?"

"Stone Allen."

Russ grimaced. "Who the heck's that?"

"Maybe you do not want to ask that question," Lela said, leaning her face in her hand. "It is a sore subject with Kay."

"It's gonna be a sore subject with me, too," Russ blurted. "I don't like last-minute surprises."

Kay shrugged. "Sorry. Wasn't my idea. Stone Allen is the

vice president of public relations for the Alyeska Consortium — and an idiot to boot."

"Stone? What kind of name is that?" Russ asked. "And what's he doin' comin' along on this trip?"

Kay folded her arms across her chest. She raised her eyebrows and rolled her eyes. "Grace said he could."

"Oh for cryin' out loud. That's all we need. A novice in the frozen Arctic doggin' our butts." Russ shook his head in disgust. "This changes things, all right. Lela, can I have that list back? We'll go over it tomorrow."

Lela surrendered the list. "Mr. Allen is going to be an interesting traveling companion, no doubt. But it seems we have no choice and must make the best of a difficult situation."

"He's convinced that we're intending to hang the oil companies out to dry," Kay explained. "And what's even more disturbing is that I think Grace wants him along so we don't do just that."

Lela looked at Kay sharply. "What?"

"Lela, you were right," Kay said with concern. "We had begun to forget about the politics involved here. I should have known better, especially after the trip Russ and I made three years ago to Prudhoe Bay. I've got a feeling our mission is to exonerate the oil companies. Or, if we do find any violations, to give them a chance to get their act together. But I guess we'll find out soon enough. I plan to report what we find — no more, no less. What happens after that won't be on our heads."

"But it will be on our consciences," Lela said. "And I wonder how any of us will handle that."

Russ cleared his throat. "Wow. Those meetings must have been humdingers."

"They were a disaster," Kay growled.

"It was not Kay's fault. Mr. Allen was not much help. He said some things that angered my people."

Kay shook her head and poked at her salad. "I thought the

place was going to erupt into a mob scene on Friday. Yesterday was a little better, but we've got our work cut out for us."

"Sounds like it," Russ agreed. "I don't like this Allen guy already. And that don't bode too well for him."

"Maybe we won't find anything out there," Kay said wistfully. "Maybe the oil companies are in total compliance with the lease agreements. It's all I can hope for now. And that's asking a lot."

Three days later, Kay sat on the floor near the fireplace, back propped up against Lela's sofa. She sipped her wine and stretched her legs toward the fire, languishing in its warmth. It had been bitterly cold the entire week, a prelude of the weather they would be facing as they set out on their journey tomorrow to Anakruak. There would be many cold nights to come in the Arctic wilderness now masked by the perpetual darkness. The roaring fire, both its warmth and its light, was a precious luxury that Kay was not in a hurry to give up.

"What are you thinking, Kay?" Lela asked, sitting down on the floor. "Are you worried about the trip?"

"No. I'll start worrying about that tomorrow." Kay chuckled. "Say, I sound just like Scarlet O'Hara."

"Yes, of course." Lela mockingly shook her fist in the air and said solemnly, "As God is my witness, I'll never eat turnips again."

Playfully, Kay squeezed Lela's arm. "I don't think that was the line exactly."

"It has been awhile since I saw the movie."

"Me, too. Actually, I wasn't thinking about the trip at all. I was enjoying this moment by the fire."

"You are relaxing then. I am glad."

"Yes, something I haven't done in quite a while. Thanks for sharing your home with me."

"It is fun for me to have company. If you live alone then you know it is not always easy."

"Tell me what happened to Robert. You said he was killed in a hunting accident."

"Yes. That is right." Lela's eyes filled with tears.

"I'm sorry, Lela. I shouldn't have asked. You don't have to talk about it."

"It is okay. It has been a long time since I told the story. It is an old one now, but when I tell it, it seems like yesterday." Lela wrapped her arms around her legs and rested her chin on her knees. "Robert was hunting whale. This is a joyful time for my people. It was summer and his hunting team was in an umiak. It is a large wooden boat covered with walrus skin. They were in the Chukchi headed north. The whale was spotted. It was a difficult kill. The spirit of the whale was strong and the boat was toppled. Robert drowned, pulled under by a strong current. Another villager also drowned."

"What a terrible tragedy."

"My people believe the spirits of the land are sometimes angry. Maybe they were angry that day."

"So you've lived alone ever since."

"Yes."

"I live alone now. My father lived with me up until a few months ago. And another friend."

Lela flashed a look of concern. "Your voice tells me that this is a cause of great unhappiness for you."

"Like I said, my father has a lot of health problems, so I had to move him into an assisted-care facility. As for my friend, there were some changes in her life and she needed to move out."

"Now I am the one who is sorry."

"Listen, I want to tell you something. It's a personal matter and doesn't really have anything to do with our professional relationship."

"Then maybe you should not tell me, Kay."

"No. I want to. It seems like we've become friends pretty quickly. You're very easy to talk to."

"That is nice of you to say."

"The friend who moved was my lover of three years. She met someone else and left me only a couple of weeks ago." Kay tried to read Lela's expression. There was no discernible change. "It's been a difficult time for me, but I think I'm okay. I mean, I'm trying to move on with my life."

"It is hard to lose someone you love no matter what the circumstances are," the soft voice replied. "It is sad that this has happened to you, Kay. I hope you can find happiness again."

"I think I'm going to take a break from relationships for now. Besides, the time alone will probably do me some good. Obviously, I still have a lot to learn when it comes to my personal life."

"What is she like?"

"Stef?"

"Yes."

Thinking about Stef, Kay couldn't help but smile. "She's a great person. It just didn't work out. There was a big age difference, and I really think that mattered for some reason. Maybe more so to me than to her." Kay threw another log onto the fire. Sparks flew, and the fire crackled around the new wood. "Stef's a free spirit. Upbeat person, always smiling, being silly. I think I was too serious for her. Always threw a wet blanket on her emotions. I can be that way."

"You no longer have your youthful exuberance?"

"Something like that. What kind of person was your husband?"

Lela wrapped a wool comforter around her shoulders. She closed her eyes as if trying to remember. "Robert was also serious about life — a lot like you. But he did have his carefree moments. His favorite time of year was spring. We have a special ceremony called the blanket toss. My people call it *nalukatak*."

72

"Yes, I've read about it. It sounds like so much fun."

"It is done to celebrate the beginning of the whale hunt, and Robert just loved it. He would talk about it for weeks before and after. It was then that the boy inside him came out. I loved to listen to him laugh."

"He must have been a wonderful person."

"He was strong on the outside, but his spirit was gentle. I felt safe with him."

"I don't think I've ever felt safe or secure with anyone, per se. I rely a lot on myself."

"Will you stay friends with Stef?"

Kay shrugged. "I hope so. But it'll be hard. I'm trying to be realistic about it. The truth is, she'll probably make new friends and, eventually, forget about me."

"It is hard for me to imagine anyone forgetting about you, Kay. People do grow apart, but for many other reasons."

"Usually it's because you take them for granted and then they meet someone else they're attracted to."

"I have never had that experience."

"You don't want to." Suddenly, Kay yawned and stretched. "Excuse me. I'm getting sleepy."

The firelight was fading. Lela got up and blew out the vanilla-scented candles on the mantel. "It will be a long day tomorrow. We should get some rest."

"Yes, the adventure finally begins."

Chapter Five

From the helicopter Kay could barely see the lights of the small native village against the white landscape, signaling their arrival at Anakruak. For the next three weeks this would be their base camp for travel into the Teshekpuk Lake region of the National Petroleum Reserve of Alaska. The helicopter touched down south of the village and Kay peered outside. In the gray darkness of that Saturday morning she could see only one main street with a jumble of cabins and prefab houses. During their three-week stay, Lela had arranged for the teams to live in two local homes. Lela, Kay, and two women from the Environmental Protection Agency would be staying in a house recently abandoned by natives who had relocated to Ikiak. The government was renting a second home, located down the street, for Russ, Allen, and four other EPA employees who would be assisting them with the investigation in the reserve.

"Everyone out," Russ yelled over the sound of the rotor blades. "Keep your heads down."

Lela jumped onto the ground and reached for Kay's hand. "It is a bit icy here. Careful."

Kay hopped out, and Stone Allen followed. Allen had been unusually quiet for most of the trip after a brief scuffle with Russ over supplies.

"What'd you say to him, Russ?" Kay asked when they had cleared the landing area.

"I told him to shut his big fat mouth and stop tellin' me how to do my job."

Kay gave Russ the thumbs-up sign. "It worked. Not a peep out of him since."

"He was workin' my last nerve, Kay. I don't know if I can survive three weeks with that guy."

"You survived several weeks with Grace Perry a few years ago."

"True. But I can make allowances for most ladies. And she may have been a pain in the butt, but she was a lady." Russ called everyone together. "Listen, I'm gonna supervise unloadin' this chopper. The pilots are headin' back to Barrow today. Lela's got the keys to the house, so you might as well follow her."

Lela walked toward the village. "One of the houses is the first one on the right."

The house was small but cozy. Lela immediately threw some wood into the fireplace. Kay inspected the rest of the rooms. There was a loft upstairs and two bedrooms on either side of the living area on the first floor. Lela had ordered two cots for each bedroom and one for the loft. The kitchen was stark with a propane stove and sink.

"This place is a dump. I hope where I'm staying is better than this," Allen complained.

Kay swung around. "If you don't like the accommodations, Allen, get back in the helicopter."

"Yes, you'd like that, I'm sure."

Lela stooped in front of the hearth and fanned the fire. "We must all make the best of this so we can finish the job we have come to do. The house that you will be staying in is much the same but will be manageable. We will all be fine."

"That's *fine* for you, lady. You live like this year-round," Allen said sharply.

Kay pointed a finger between Allen's eyes. "Don't you ever talk to anyone on this team like that again or you'll be out of here. And I mean it."

"I'm here as long as Washington wants me here. And trust me, Westmore, they want me here."

The front door opened and Russ lumbered in, ushered by a cold, harsh wind. "Okay, the supplies and your own personal belongings are stacked outside. The snowmobiles are already parked out back of the house."

"Where's the house we're staying in, Bend? I want to get going." Allen headed toward the door.

Russ blocked the door with his arm. "Listen, buster, you're not goin' anywhere. We've still got some work to do."

"In a hurry, Allen?" Kay asked.

Allen sneered. "I've got some work to do if none of you mind."

Kay nodded in agreement. "Yes, you do. And it's right here, so listen up. Lela and I will take the front room. The other two ladies from EPA can take the loft and the back room. I think that'll make us all comfortable enough."

Russ ushered the group outside. "Sounds like a good setup. There's plenty of room for you ladies."

"Fine. Let's get to work then." Kay grabbed a duffel bag. "We've got to get all these supplies and equipment stowed inside. Weather's going be lousy tonight. Better tomorrow. All the supplies we're taking with us into the reserve have to be packed according to Russ's instructions. Then we're going to have a meeting over lunch to discuss exactly what's happening tomorrow."

About twenty minutes later, Kay sat down on the cot in the front bedroom and rooted through her clothes for a heavy sweater. Slipping it over her head, she strolled into the kitchen, where Russ was mixing tuna and mayonnaise. "Are you going to be chief cook and bottle washer, too?" she asked, grabbing some sodas from the refrigerator.

"Hey, I'll do whatever. I'm not proud."

"I think you're right about Allen. I may have to kill him before all this is over."

"Get in line."

"How the hell did he ever get into the public relations field? He's acerbic, confrontational, and a total moron."

"Can't argue with you, Kay. But we didn't have much choice in the matter."

"No, once again we got screwed. I've been thinking about how tomorrow's going to pan out. Any guesses?"

"I just hope we can get through day one without any major incidents. Like me runnin' Junior over with my snowmobile."

Kay got hysterical. "Junior? That's good."

"I swear that guy doesn't even shave yet."

"When are the EPA folks arriving?"

"They're flyin' in tomorrow morning at seven. Team of six. Four guys, two ladies. The ladies are chemical experts. They'll be helpin' you and Lela conduct the water testing. The guys are land surveyors, and they'll be comin' along with me and Junior."

The group sat quietly in the living room eating tuna sandwiches and munching Ruffles potato chips while Kay outlined Sunday's itinerary. "The entire team, including our friends from EPA, will head south by snowmobile along the eastern shores of Teshekpuk Lake. At the three-mile mark,

Dawn Jeffries and Michelle Gere of the EPA, myself and Lela will turn off from the main trail to the eastern lake shore." Kay traced the trail on a topographical map. "We'll do our first water tests about here to look for any suspicious trace chemicals associated with petroleum products. Russ, Allen, David Carter, Tom Williams, Robert Goddard, and Albert Gonzalez of EPA will continue south. There's some drilling and testing being done by a couple of the oil companies south of the lake. At the drilling site, the guys will conduct some land surveying to make sure the oil companies are confining their operations to the lease area. The team will also check for any illegal chemicals or dumps."

"I've arranged for some oil company surveyors to meet us there," Allen said. "Want to make sure we all get the same results."

Kay bristled when she heard this. "Next time I'd appreciate being properly informed of any plans you make, Allen. You know, we could at least try to work together on this."

"The government doesn't want to work with us," Allen commented sullenly.

"You're here, aren't you?" Kay replied. "That speaks for itself. I repeat, let's try to work together on this." Kay folded the map. "After we return tomorrow, Lela's going to interview some of the residents of Anakruak. A lot of the complaints about oil-company lease violations have come from Anakruak and Alaktak."

"I'll want to sit in on those interviews," Allen demanded.

"No problem." Lela smiled politely and handed Allen a booklet. "But you must first brush up on your Inupiaq. The native residents will not speak to us in English."

"Oh great. And how do I know the translations will be made accurately and fairly?"

"Why wouldn't they be?" Kay snapped.

"You tell me."

"Listen, no one's going to communicate any inaccurate

information." Kay slammed her briefcase shut. "This is an official government investigation. We leave at eight in the morning. Right now, Lela and I are going to take a walk through Anakruak."

A condescending smirk crossed Allen's face. "That'll take about five minutes."

"Yeah, and while they're doin' that you can help me pack the supplies for tomorrow's trip," Russ said, getting up from the table. "We're also gonna fire up the snowmobiles. Make sure they're in runnin' order."

Outside, Kay could barely control her temper. "That guy's a first-rate ass, excuse my French. I want to wipe that smirk right off his face."

"He does work the nerves," Lela agreed.

"I don't know why I always have to make these trips with inexperienced bureaucrats. I must've done something wrong as a kid." Kay kicked at the snow. "I want to try to work with this guy, but he won't budge an inch."

"Life tests us in many ways."

"No, Grace tests me."

"You and Grace do not get along?"

"Well, it's kind of a love-hate relationship, let's put it that way."

"You have much resolve, Kay. You will be fine."

"I'm glad you're here. I need your steadiness."

"You have it whenever you need it."

The snow-covered lane, dividing one row of village homes from the other, ran to the edge of a large icy slope and ended as abruptly as it began. Most of the traffic along the small thoroughfare was made on foot, dogsled, or snowmobile.

"This makes Barrow look cosmopolitan," Kay said to Lela as they approached the end of the lane. "But it's quiet and beautiful. I could get used to life like this."

"Without bureaucrats?"

"Exactly."

"When you look at this isolated village you can understand

why the Teshekpuk Lake area is vital to our people. It is what sustains them here in this wilderness." Lela glanced over her shoulder at a group of men two houses down. With their oil lamps casting an eerie glow in the darkness, they meticulously prepared their dogsleds and fed their animals. "Most of the villagers fish and hunt. Those men are preparing to ice fish. If they are lucky they will also kill a bear. They have stored food for the winter, but the fight for survival never ends."

"Do they know why we're here?"

"They know exactly who we are and why we are here. Their village council approved our visit and stay. I flew down myself to attend the meeting."

"We didn't exactly get the brass-band greeting."

"Did we need one?"

Kay studied Lela's face. The expression was tranquil, eyes betraying only a hint of confusion. Things were simple for Lela and that's how she viewed the world, Kay had learned. She admired Lela's sense of validation that came from herself and not from others. To the contrary, Kay was always struggling for acceptance from her family, friends, and colleagues. Smiling broadly, Kay finally answered the question. "No, we didn't need a brass band greeting. So long as we're not a disruption or concern to them — that's all that matters."

"If we become a concern, they will be the first to let us know."

"Good. Then we'll just go about our business as they seem to be going about theirs."

Though bitterly cold, Sunday morning arrived without any precipitation. The EPA teams landed on time and quickly introduced themselves. After a brief chat, all hands pitched in to pack the equipment the EPA teams needed on their snowmobiles. Twenty minutes later, they were underway, the roar of the snowmobile engines pleasantly muffled by Kay's helmet. Kay followed Russ, the glare of headlights barely keeping him in view. Lela was directly behind Kay. The EPA team was next, and Allen brought up the rear, which Kay felt was entirely appropriate. The trail was rutted and icy. It was so bad that Kay's insides felt like they'd been put through a Mixmaster. Twice she almost lost control of the snowmobile and her hands began to cramp from gripping the machine so tightly.

Kay's headset crackled. It was Russ. "Kay, you reading me?"

"Yeah. I hear you fine."

"The lake's to our right now — about three thousand yards. You can peel off anytime. Our team will meet you at exactly four o'clock at the Kogru River landing strip. Roger?"

"Roger. See you later. Out."

Kay called Lela, Dawn, and Michelle from the built-in headset. When she heard the affirmative replies from all of the women crackling in her ears, she made a slow turn from the trail toward the line of evergreens that bordered the lakeshore. As instructed, the rest of the team followed her. Ten minutes later the glow of their headlights broke through the maze of trees. What Kay saw was a vast open space in an otherwise featureless landscape. She tried to imagine that same space in summer — an oasis of blue with moose and caribou drinking from the lakeshores. Parking the snow-mobiles under the shelter of snow-draped pines, they all peered into the morning darkness. A cold wind whipped at their faces and howled across the frozen lake like a lonely wolf. Kay removed her helmet and stepped into her snow-shoes, strapping them tightly around her boots. Through the thin Polartec mask that protected her face, she could feel the frigid air burning her skin. It was hard to breathe. She snapped on a pair of clear goggles to protect her eyes. Lela, Dawn, and Michele had already started to unpack the equipment.

Inside the line of trees, the women set up two tents. Though they only planned to work in that area a few hours, they would need frequent breaks from the cold. Kay equipped each tent with a portable white-gas heater for relief from the frigid air.

The surface of the lake was covered with at least a foot of frozen snow. "It could be worse," Lela said wryly, sweeping the ground with a flashlight. "Three feet is not uncommon."

Dawn unlatched a large, black case. "Yes, we've tested water in worse conditions than these. Just last month we were working in the Gates of the Arctic reserve and got stuck for a week in a blizzard. All because some self-proclaimed environmental terrorist was threatening to poison the area with benzene."

"Did you find this terrorist?" Lela asked.

"No. But we found some drums of benzene. Very scary stuff. It can pass through the soil into underground water. And if it gets dumped into a water supply, it breaks down slowly. The stuff can poison a bunch of people in no time."

"We think the guy's threats were real," Michelle added. "Fortunately, he didn't get time to play his deadly game. Of course, 'he' could be an organized group. Some crazy environmental terrorist network. It's a new kind of terrorism — the kind that can cause panic over a widespread area in one strike."

Rummaging through her equipment, Dawn seemed unconcerned. "The government's already investigating the dump. Our sources think it was an isolated case, thank goodness."

"Benzene? That is a very dangerous substance," Lela said with concern. "It is a carcinogen and would cause far worse damage to the land and our people than any oil spill I can think of."

"That's true," Michelle agreed. "It's comforting to know it was an isolated incident."

"I'm sure the EPA won't take anything for granted with a

threat like that," Kay said while sliding the power auger from its leather enclosure. "Where would you guys like to begin?"

"Over there," Michelle pointed, a few of her blond curls spilling out from underneath her hood. "The land slopes gradually here. A good place to test for any chemical runoff."

"Let's get started then," Kay agreed. The women erected two high-amp aluminum light poles. As soon as they could see, Kay strode onto the frozen surface of the lake and pressed the auger's primer bulb. With the small, silver key she turned the ignition over. The auger roared and spun on the first attempt. "Thank God for electronic ignition," she yelled to the women, smiling.

Dawn, Michelle, and Lela stood a few yards away, water-testing kits and other supplies tucked under their arms. They watched as Kay throttled up the auger. Snow flew everywhere as she eased the auger into position. In a clockwise spin, the machine quickly cut through the softer snow. Kay could feel some resistance as she hit ice for the first time. The ice was about three inches thick, but the power of the auger broke through in only a few minutes. Kay cut the engine and stepped back.

"That's it. We're through."

Lela shook her head in amazement. "Modern technology is a wonderful thing. It sometimes takes a good hour for my people to cut through the ice to fish. Every native family should have one of those."

Kay idled the auger and then shut it down. "Russ knows the best equipment. He's a genius."

Carefully, Michelle and Dawn chopped loose snow away from the edge of the ice with small pick hammers. Opening the water-testing field kits, they arranged chemicals and test tubes and went to work.

"What exactly are we testing for, ladies?" Kay asked, stooping down next to them.

"This kit does nine basic water-quality tests," Michelle explained. "We'll check levels of alkalinity, ammonia, carbon dioxide, dissolved oxygen, pH, iron, and some other measurements. From these tests we should be able to determine if any chemicals have been dumped in the lake or have run off from nearby work areas. Of course we'll have to conduct a number of tests in the area to make sure the levels of all of these agents are consistent and where they should be."

Dawn and Michelle filled the clear plastic tubes with water, adding the various chemical agents as necessary. This procedure lasted about ten minutes. In the meantime, Kay drilled about five other sites. Lela followed close behind with reflective orange cones to mark the positions. These sites were also tested. An hour later, as the two women finally packed their supplies in weatherproof cases, Kay thought she might keel over from the cold.

"Hey, let's head for the tents. I'm dying out here." Kay killed the lights and grabbed the auger, heading toward shelter. She got no argument from anyone else.

The women had hooked the two tents together. Opening the main flap, Kay crawled inside. She peeled the Polartec mask off and felt the welcome warmth. Her face began to tingle from the change in temperature.

Lela unpacked a Bunsen burner. "Who will have some tea or coffee?"

Removing her headgear, Dawn revealed sea-green eyes and hair as dark as the eternal Alaskan night. "Sounds great. Coffee for me."

Michelle slipped off her boots and rubbed her toes. "I'll have some coffee. This constant night is driving me nuts. All I want to do is sleep." She stretched out along the tunnel that joined the two tents and let out a huge yawn. "After our trip to the Gates of the Arctic, Dawn and I were in Nome doing some field tests at an old petroleum dump. After two weeks of working in the dark, I think I've become a caffeine addict."

Lela held a match to the Bunsen burner. The gas burst into flames with an audible *whoosh*. "In the summer, when there is no night, it is just as much of an adjustment, too. But after many years, your body gets used to it."

"Think I could get used to summers here. Long days and bright sunshine. What could be more perfect?" Dawn opened a bag of pretzels and passed them around. "Endless summers in Alaska. Another reason why Alaska's like no other place on earth."

"You think we're going to find any infractions here?" Michelle sipped her coffee, warming her hands with the hot cup. "Teshekpuk Lake. Man, that's no place to mess with. I'm surprised the government ever let the oil companies near here."

Kay rolled over on her side and propped herself up with her elbow. "It's all politics. Big money. It's never the land or the people or the future. It's corporate interests and government deals. Pressure from foreign governments or threats from terrorists. Complaints from environmental groups or energy lobbies. You never know what form the enemy is going to take. Leasing the lands nearby should have been a safe deal. But everyone has to hold up their end of the bargain."

"That is what we are here to find out," Lela said. "Who is holding up their end of the bargain and who is not."

Kay retied her boots. "Yes. We'll find that out soon enough. Enjoy your break, ladies. Another fifteen minutes, then we've got to move again."

Four hours later, Kay and the crew had tested ten different locations along the lake's eastern shore. In the process of redistributing some equipment along the frozen tractor trail, all heads turned toward the south as a caravan of oil company trucks, motors cranking roughly in the frigid air, made its way north to Anakruak. As the lead truck in the caravan approached the group of women standing next to their snowmobiles, it slowed and then stopped. One by one the trucks following behind also stopped, idling their engines, puffs of gray engine smoke trailing into the darkness.

The second vehicle's driver-side door opened, and a short, stocky man wearing a blue hard hat and goggles stepped out. A few minutes later, all the truck doors were open and a group of workers huddled nearby. The man in the blue hat and black wilderness boots struggled through the snow until he stopped a few feet away.

Kay watched the man's chest rise and fall beneath his parka. He had only walked a few yards, but the snow was high and the air bitter. Her stomach tightened and she licked her lips, wondering if there was going to be an unpleasant confrontation.

"Do you ladies need help?" he said in a friendly tone.

"No. We're just making some adjustments to our equipment," Kay answered calmly. "But thanks for asking."

"Name's John Wilson. We're with the oil consortium. Been setting up a drill bed down south."

"Kay Westmore, Department of the Interior."

"Oh right. We heard the government was going to be in the area. Make sure we're behaving ourselves." Wilson laughed and flipped up his goggles. "You know, we've got about a million maps telling us where not to be."

"I'm sure you do." Kay glanced back toward the lake. "We just finished testing the water at Teshekpuk."

"That must have been a job. But the weather's sure been holding for you."

"Hey!" a voice yelled. "We drilled a hole in the ice yesterday and pissed in the lake. Hope that doesn't screw up your results!"

The comment was followed by laughter. Then another voice said, "Hey, I took a dump in the lake. That gonna be a problem?" More laughter.

As though ready to say something, Dawn stepped forward out of the shadows. Kay reached and grabbed Dawn's shoulder, squeezing it reassuringly.

Wilson shrugged, seemingly unconcerned. "Don't mind the boys. It's been a long day. They're just kidding around."

"No offense taken," Kay answered through her teeth. "We're just doing our jobs too."

Wilson turned and waved his hand. His crew broke up and started back to their vehicles. "You ladies be careful. Headed back to Anakruak?"

"No, the Kogru River landing area."

"Well, good luck."

"You, too."

The women stood quietly while the trucks moved slowly up the ice-covered trail. When the vehicles finally disappeared, Kay inwardly breathed a huge sigh of relief. It was a relatively benign encounter.

"I thought things were going to get ugly," Lela said. "The tension was thicker than this cold air."

Kay nodded. "Word has certainly spread that we're working in the area."

"Seems like the crew leader was an okay guy," Michelle said. "That was lucky."

Dawn kicked angrily at the snow. "Assholes. They think they own this tundra."

"We've put up with their crap before, and I'm sure this won't be the last time." Kay turned back toward the snowmobiles. "Guess we better get going. Russ'll be waiting for us."

Now, as the landscape sped past in a blur of white, Kay struggled to follow the winter trail to the Kogru River landing strip. The weather was still clear and the stars were out, but the darkness, combined with the rough trail and fatigue, made the excursion even more treacherous. Kay's headset crackled in her ears. "Kay, I am having problems with the snowmobile. I must stop," Lela's voice said, betraying some concern.

"Roger that, Lela. We'll stop right away." Kay radioed the other women and explained the situation. She sighed heavily and wondered what else could go wrong. Pulling over, she let the engine idle and headed toward Lela's snowmobile. "Hey, what's up?" Kay asked Lela through the headset. The wind shear had increased, making it impossible for them to remove their headgear.

Lela rubbed the gas gauge with her thumb. "The engine keeps cutting out. There is plenty of gas, so it has to be something else."

"It's nothing we can fix here. We'll have to repack the equipment and leave the snowmobile. You can ride with me," Kay instructed. She motioned to Dawn and Michelle to begin redistributing the equipment from Lela's snowmobile to the others. Ten minutes later, they were underway again.

"I have to admit, this is a lot nicer," Lela said over the headset. "You make a great wind block, Kay." Her arms were wrapped tightly around Kay's waist, her head buried against Kay's back.

Kay let her arm drop for a second, patting Lela's leg. "I'm glad I'm useful for something." It felt good to have someone's arms around her again for whatever reason, Kay thought. As the women continued in an easterly direction, Kay's mind wandered back to that first spring when she had met Stef.

After a bitter breakup with a former lover, Kay had finally gathered the nerve to venture out again. It was a party at a friend's house along the Chena River. When she arrived that afternoon, she said an awkward hello to a dozen or more friends she hadn't seen during the months of her self-imposed seclusion. There were many hugs and exclamations of "Where have you been?"

Her friend, Sharon, who was hosting the party, saved her from further inquisition by shepherding her to the nearest dock, where several women sat, enjoying the unseasonably warm weather. "Oh, Kay, this is Stef Kramer. I don't think you've met."

"Hi ya. Nice to meet you," the voice behind Kay said.

Kay swung back toward the bank and was immediately slammed by the vision of sun-white blond hair, eyes the color of fresh pine needles, a smile that was unmistakably happy. The smile touched Kay like nothing had in some time.

"Hungry?" Stef asked, blocking the sun with her hand.

"Yes," Kay said softly. "Yes, I am."

"Then follow me." Stef turned, her small frame connected by curves that ran smooth like the water below them. Kay shuffled behind, suddenly conscious of her larger frame. Muscled from miles of walking. Running. Carrying backpacks loaded with equipment. Seeming so clumsy now. Hulking and unattractive. Well, what of it? It would hardly matter to this young woman. She was just being nice to an older, heartbroken dyke. Sharon had probably talked to her, wanting Kay to have some company during a difficult return to socializing.

"Do you live in Fairbanks?" Kay asked.

"Yes, I'm a student at the university. Live on campus. You?"

"Lived here all my life."

"What's your job?"

"I'm a ranger with the National Park Service."

Stef's eyes brightened. "How exciting!"

Stef directed Kay to the food. After they each filled their plates, they headed back down to the water.

"Let's sit near that big spruce," Stef pointed. "It's sunny and warm there."

Sitting at the water's edge in the heat of the sun, Kay mostly listened as Stef talked about herself, her family, school.

She found herself basking, not only in the sun, but also in this young woman's gentleness. And she laughed as Stef's easy humor soothed the festering wounds that had, for uncounted days, incapacitated her. She stared at Stef closely, wondering if she'd known her for months instead of minutes.

". . . anyway, I ended up sliding down the slope on my butt. It was the first time I'd ever been skiing." Stef slapped her thigh and laughed. "Oh my God, I've been blithering on like a little idiot. I'm sorry."

"That's okay. I'm enjoying it."

Stef reached for Kay's hand, squeezing it lightly. "Do you ever go out for a beer or anything?"

Kay shrugged. The sudden contact with Stef threw her off guard. "Once in a while. Not very much lately."

"Do you have a girlfriend?"

"Not anymore."

"Maybe you'd like to have dinner some time."

"Sure. Why not?" As soon as she answered, Kay wondered where the words had come from. Stef couldn't be any more than twenty-one or -two. What kind of disaster was she setting herself up for? It was entirely too soon for this. Kay wrapped her arms around her knees. "But, then again, maybe not."

Stef's shoulders drooped, her eyes questioning the sudden change of heart. "Why?"

"I'm just not ready yet. For dating, I mean. It's too soon. But I'm very flattered that you asked. Thank you."

"Well, that doesn't mean you can't make new friends, does it?"

Kay thought about that question. The answer seemed obvious. "No."

"And you have dinner with friends, don't you?"

"Sure."

"Good. How 'bout this Friday?"

Kay laughed. She'd been artfully snookered. "Friday would be fine."

Stef lay on her side, the roundness of her breasts, the curve of her hips, the smooth tanned thighs sending Kay's mind on a frantic search for some kind of centeredness.

"By the way," Stef said softly. "I think you're the sexiest woman I've ever met."

Kay gripped the grass on either side of her, fingernails cutting through the grass into her palms. "Thank you. But I think I should be saying that to you."

"Then why don't you?"

"Because if I do, I won't be able to stop myself."

Stef rolled over, ending up next to Kay, her shoulder blade resting on top of Kay's hand. "Stop yourself from doing what?"

Kay could feel the softness of Stef's breast against her forearm. She looked down at the pristine face, high cheekbones chiseled beneath sun-pinkened skin. "From making a complete and utter fool of myself."

A cross wind blasted the open flats, hitting the snowmobile on the left side, blowing the vehicle's rear end into a skid. The strength of the wind caused the snowmobile to handle like it was made of tin. Kay fought for control on the already unstable trail. She turned into the first skid and then leaned into the next. Seconds later, she maneuvered the machine back to the middle of the trail. Kay glanced over her shoulder and saw Dawn and Michelle still following safely behind.

"Hang on tight," Kay said to Lela. "This is getting interesting."

"I have no plans to let go."

Please don't, Kay thought. Suddenly, consciously, and for the first time Kay acknowledged her growing attraction to Lela. *Absurd* was the only word that riddled her mind after that. *Absurd*. Lela lived in Barrow, hundreds of miles away, had been married for many years and hadn't shown the slightest interest in Kay beyond friendship. I'm doing it again, she thought. Being stupid. Kay felt Lela's arms clutching her waist, the weight of Lela's shoulders against her back. A twinge in her stomach caused her to sigh heavily. Once again, it was too soon. And, once again, there was the danger of making a complete and utter fool of herself.

Fours days later, after testing the water at more than forty locations around the lake, Kay led the team back to the Kogru airfield for yet another rendezvous with Russ and crew. The airfield was an oasis in the frozen landscape. Its heated airstrip was a stark, black stripe on a field of white. Even in the darkness the airstrip was visible — blacker than the night and out of place in this world of ice and snow.

As usual, Russ and his crew were huddled inside a small outbuilding that normally served as a shelter for mechanics, pilots, and emergency personnel. Kay headed straight for Russ, needing the comfort of her friend to keep her on an even keel.

"How did it go today?" she asked, resting her hand on his shoulder.

"Pretty good. I think we're about finished with the south and west work sites. Between tomorrow and next week we can finish off the north and east. Then we'll have all the data we need. I gotta tell you, Kay, so far I haven't seen any blatant problems or violations." Russ pulled her to the side. "Idiot Brain caused me more headaches today." Russ nodded toward Stone Allen. "This mornin' all Junior did was whine and moan about where we placed our equipment, that our leasing maps were inaccurate, you name it. Demands to compare our data to his data. Which brings up another issue. His boys from the oil companies have been about as obnoxious as bulls in the ring every damned day we've been out there."

"They weren't too friendly to us the first day out. I'm

thankful we haven't gotten too close since then to have any more unfriendly chats."

"There's more activity where we are. And when I got back to the main tents this afternoon, I found some of our equipment damaged. Bludgeoned to hell to be more accurate."

"Sabotage?"

"Yeah, if you mean our equipment got the shit beat out of it. Then that's exactly the word I'd use."

"Do you think Allen had anything to do with it?"

"Not directly. I haven't let his ass outta my sight for one minute during this entire trip. I've watched him like a hawk for four days, just hopin' he'd give me an excuse to send him packin'."

"Okay. We'll meet in the morning and make some re-assessments. I take it the copter should be here shortly."

"Yeah, any minute. They radioed about a half-hour ago. The wind's a little rough again today, but nothing they can't manage."

"Good. Quite frankly, I'm beat. Not to mention the fact that my insides feel like Jell-O."

"I hear ya, boss. I'm ready for a quiet night and a nice warm beer."

"*Warm* beer? Sounds great." Kay chuckled, enjoying the good laugh. "Let's get out of here."

In Anakruak, at the end of the one-road village, there was a small bar decorated with caribou antlers, a variety of animal skins, fishing nets, and other hunting implements unrecognizable to Kay. This Thursday evening the bar was like it was on any other weekday evening — noisy and filled with smoke. The customers were mostly native. A few Caucasian males Kay suspected were oil workers sat at a table in the far corner of the room drinking beer. Kay, Russ, and Lela, along with the rest of the EPA team, had made the bar their nightly haunt. After the end of each day, they needed desperately to unwind. The group pushed their two usual tables together and collapsed into their respective chairs. They ordered pitchers of beer and smoked-salmon burgers. Bleary-eyed and muscles aching, Kay intended to stay only for about an hour. Tomorrow would be another long day taking water samples from the northern and western lakeshores.

Sitting next to Kay, Lela raised her beer mug. "Here is to another safe and successful day. It is always good to come out of the wilderness without harm. Sometimes the spirits of the land are not always so kind. Today they were once again peaceful."

Kay clinked her glass against Lela's. "Well, we lost a snowmobile earlier this week. But that's the least of my worries. You're right, Lela. So long as we get back safe every day, that's all that matters. Thanks to everyone for all your help."

"Spirits of the land? Do you really believe that bunk?" Allen asked, already on his second beer. He had a penchant for downing four or five beers a night, becoming slightly more obnoxious with each one under his belt.

"Listen, if you're gonna be uncivil-like again, go to another table," Russ suggested hotly. "It's time to take a load off and quit the crap. It's been a long week, and it ain't over yet."

"Don't get your nose out of joint, Bend. I was just asking the lady a question." Allen gulped his beer. "This Eskimo culture is pretty fascinating stuff."

"Well, Mr. Allen, I can only say this." Lela folded her hands in front of her and talked in a firm, even tone. "There is an old Inupiat saying that goes something like this. 'I will walk with leg muscles, which are strong as the sinews of the shins of the little caribou calf. I will walk with leg muscles, which are strong as the sinews of the shins of the little hare. I will take care not to go toward the dark. I will go toward the day.' "

Allen flashed a recognizable sneer. "What's all that supposed to mean?"

"It means, Mr. Allen, that you should remember we are one team here. And that you should take care not to offend because should you accidentally walk toward the dark, there may not be anyone around to help you back toward the day."

The entire group snickered.

"Was that some kind of threat or something?"

"No, Mr. Allen. It was merely some advice. Or what did you call it? Bunk?"

For the next half-hour Allen sulked quietly. Russ began telling the EPA team old National Park Service adventure stories that Kay had already heard or experienced firsthand. Kay took the opportunity to chat quietly with Lela. It was an intimate conversation that transcended the bar's more raucous atmosphere. The bar was full now with the booming voices of many Inupiat men back from the day's hunt.

"In Fairbanks, are your friends mostly women, Kay?"

Kay smiled. "Mostly. But not all. Russ is a dear friend whom I just happen to work with. I have some other male acquaintances as well."

"I do not have many close friends. When my husband died and I decided to go back to school, Robert's family wanted nothing more to do with me."

"That's pretty sad."

"It is. But that is the way with the Inupiat. Life for a woman is to be with her family and nothing more. Did I tell you?" Lela poured Kay another mug of beer. "About six months after Robert died his family wanted to fix me up with his brother."

"Really?"

"Yes. One day his entire family arrived on my doorstep unannounced, older brother in tow."

"Kind of insensitive, if you ask me."

"To them it was a permissible intervention on my behalf.

Ordained by the spirits and meant to bring me back into the tribe. They also brought the tribal shaman."

"Shaman?"

"Yes, shaman's are like ministers. They are consulted to heal illnesses and resolve serious problems. I was the serious problem."

Kay rested her chin in her hand. "I never would have thought that about you, Lela. What happened?"

"They sat and stared at me, and I stared back. I did not know what in the world to do. Besides, Robert's brother was quite a bit older and had already been married two times. I was to be wife number three."

"Good grief."

Lela giggled softly. "Thaddeus, Robert's brother . . ."

"*Thaddeus?* You're joking."

"No — a family name and a long story. At any rate, Thaddeus was about five-foot-eleven and three hundred pounds. A huge man by Inupiat standards, with the biggest hands I have ever seen and a bulldog face. Kay, it scared the hell out of me just to look at him."

Kay burst out laughing, and Lela joined in. "So, obviously it wasn't just going to law school that pissed them off."

"No. It was also the wounded pride of a brother."

"Being wife number three would have been more than a bit much for me."

"My thoughts exactly." Lela rubbed her shoulder and winced. "Must have pulled a muscle in my shoulder or something. It is feeling very stiff."

Kay was about to respond when she heard loud voices and a scuffle. The Caucasian oil workers had migrated from the table in the far corner of the room and were now standing toe to toe with a group of natives near the bar. The natives were yelling in Inupiaq, and the oil workers were screaming back in English. Someone kicked a chair, and a barstool fell over.

There was some shoving and jostling of bodies, and beer started to fly. The next sound Kay heard was a loud explosion. Lela reached over and yanked Kay to the floor.

"What the hell was that?" Kay asked as she hit the wooden floor with an audible thump.

"A rifle shot," Lela said, crouching next to Kay. "The natives are definitely restless tonight." She smiled and squeezed Kay's hand. "You see, my people can also be short-tempered."

"No wonder I fit in so well here."

Another shot rang out and, with a loud stampede of footsteps, the crowd vaporized in an instant. When Kay finally mustered enough courage to lift her head, she spied the owner of the business standing behind the bar, rifle raised arrow-straight in the air. Except for Kay's group and a few other patrons who had also hit the deck, the room was empty. Kay got up and searched for everyone in her group. Other than some wide-eyed stares, no one appeared to be hurt.

"I am sorry, Kay," Lela said. "I hope I did not hurt you. I meant only to get you down on the floor."

Kay chuckled. "Well, next time you want to wrestle me to the floor, Lela, there are nicer ways to do it."

Lela blushed and put her hand to her face. "I am sorry. Unfortunately, I have been in situations like this before."

"Damned Eskimos can never hold their liquor," Allen muttered, dusting off his trousers.

Russ huffed a response. "Seems like those oil workers weren't handlin' themselves real well either. In ten minutes, I'll be in bed. That little stunt took the last starch outta me."

"Everyone else okay?" Kay asked. They nodded their heads meekly. Kay glanced over toward the bar and left the owner more than enough money to pay the bill and tip.

~ ~ ~ ~ ~

In the darkness of their small room, Kay could hear Lela breathing. The two uncomfortable cots were shoved parallel to one another about two feet apart. The room was so cramped that Kay could reach out and touch the pale wooden dresser to her immediate left. It was the only other piece of furniture in the room.

Kay stared at the ceiling and thought about the last six days. So much had happened that she couldn't help wondering what tomorrow would bring. Suddenly, Lela spoke and jolted her from her thoughts.

"What happened at the bar tonight — it is unfortunately not an uncommon thing."

"Really? Scared the hell out of me. I don't like guns."

"We are a peaceful people, but the firing of guns seems to be a form of expression we have adopted. The Inupiat shoot outside their houses on New Year's Eve or down at the sea when the ice flows begin to break apart in summer. A rifle to a young native boy is like a baseball bat to a Caucasian child."

"Why the emphasis on guns?"

"It is all wrapped up in the importance of the hunt. To be a good hunter is to be a success. So when trouble starts, Inupiat men reach for the gun, too. Especially young men who know of nothing else. The only good thing is that we do not usually end up shooting each other. The gun is used to warn and protect. And sometimes to celebrate."

After weeks of perennial blackness, Kay's eyes had grown accustomed to seeing in the dark. To her right, she could see Lela lying on her side, clutching her left shoulder.

"Lela, is your shoulder still bothering you?"

"Yes. A dull throb."

"Let me take a look at it."

Lela sat up, her feet dangling from the cot. She was wearing a large T-shirt with long underwear underneath. "I must have hurt it when I was unloading some of the equipment earlier today. But it did not start to bother me until late this afternoon. It is really just old age, I think."

"Well, I'll politely dispute the old-age comment, and I can't promise a cure. But I'm certified in first aid and I've been told that I give great backrubs."

"And who was it that told you that?"

Kay felt herself blushing and was glad for the darkness. "Some old friends."

"I see. Then I am at your mercy."

Kay sat on Lela's cot and gently rotated the arm sideways and up and down. "Painful?"

"A little."

She began to lightly massage the shoulder and Lela suddenly relaxed. Kay could feel the tension in the shoulder easing. "Feeling stressed about anything in particular?"

"Maybe. I do not really know. This job right now, and maybe what we will find in the reserve is stressful enough."

"That's true. Anything else?"

"Offhand, nothing that I can think of. Why do you ask?"

"I think the problem with your shoulder is mostly tension."

"What you are doing feels good."

"I'm glad." Kay continued the gentle massage, kneading her fingers into Lela's shoulder. Suddenly, she wondered what it would be like to kiss Lela. And then just as quickly she admonished herself. What are you thinking? Are you crazy? She tried to concentrate on anything else, but her mind kept wandering back to the long raven hair, silky against her hands. Kay followed the line of Lela's neck as it softly curved down to her shoulders.

Flashes of Stef flew into her mind, along with the hurt of having lost her. The humiliation of the recent months came back — the constant fight to keep her emotions intact as she listened while Stef packed, leaving the apartment to be with another woman. But even those thoughts didn't seem to deter her. Somehow she managed to push the fear away, if only for a second.

Leaning down, she brushed the hair away from Lela's neck and kissed the soft skin between the hairline and shoulder blade. Lela jumped and startled Kay to her senses. Kay shot up and stood there in the dark between the two cots, adrenaline coursing through her veins.

"I . . . I'm sorry," she stuttered. "I don't know what I was thinking. My God . . ."

Lela just sat there and said nothing while Kay continued to panic.

"Please . . . forgive me. I didn't mean —"

Lela stood a few inches away. "Mean it? You did not mean the kiss?"

"I only meant that . . . that I shouldn't have. It was totally inappropriate. What you must be thinking. Lord knows, I don't know what I was thinking."

"I am thinking I wish you would not have stopped. I am also thinking that I wish you would kiss me again."

Kay felt like she'd been kicked in the gut. For a moment, the breath went out of her and the room began to spin. She sat down to steady herself.

"Lela, I'm sorry. I don't know what to say. It was spontaneous. It just happened."

"Happened because you have feelings for me or because you are naturally spontaneous?"

Kay smiled. "Obviously, I have feelings for you."

Lela knelt in front of Kay. "Say that you will put your arms around me. That you will kiss me again. I have feelings for you, too, Kay. I think from the first moment we met."

"I think we're both tired. I know I am. We should get some rest."

Rising to her feet, Lela said softly, "Yes, you are right. We have another long day tomorrow."

Kay stretched out, her heart thumping in her chest.

Taking some deep breaths, she tried to calm herself. Then she felt a hand wrap around her own.

"Kay, it is all right." Lela squeezed her hand tightly. "Go to sleep. There is nothing to worry about."

Kay fell asleep holding Lela's hand.

The next morning, Kay waited patiently in the kitchen for Stone Allen. Russ and the rest of the team members were having breakfast down the street at the other house. Kay requested the meeting because of the continual problems Russ and the EPA teams were experiencing with Allen and the oil company workers south of the lake.

Allen strode into the room, his face shadowed by the stubble of a new beard. "What's up, Westmore?"

"Good morning."

Allen sat down and began cleaning his nails with a toothpick. "Morning."

"Listen, Russ filled me in on some things that have been happening."

"Like what?"

"Like damaged equipment. Interference by you that's delaying the work of the EPA team. Missing field reports that will result in more survey work."

"Are you accusing me of this stuff?"

"I'm telling you what I know. Why don't you tell me what you know."

"I don't know what you're talking about."

"Listen, this investigation is going to come to a close no matter what. I don't care if it takes another three months. And you can delay our work and make it more difficult but that won't change the outcome."

"An outcome that will damage the reputations of the oil companies?"

"I don't know that to be true. Do you?"

"The oil companies are in compliance."

"Then why don't you cooperate? Why do you insist on making my job more difficult?"

"Because my clients are trying to run a business. The government has no right to interfere with that."

"This land belongs to the citizens of Alaska, not to the oil companies. That's why the government's involved."

"This discussion is pointless. I want this investigation to end as quickly as you do. But I'm sure the oil company workers who are busting their butts out there in the freezing cold don't feel the same way. Maybe they're sick of the government poking their noses into everything. If they happen to make your job a bit more difficult, I imagine that's a small victory to them."

"Give them a message for me."

"What?"

"Tell them we haven't found any infractions to this point. Tell them we hope not to find any. We're here to clear them so they can continue their work, and that's the honest truth."

"I'm not a government spokesperson. Tell them yourself."

The drilling sites south of the lake were a mass of heavy equipment, temporary storage areas, and trailers to house the workers. Kay stared at the giant drilling rig crisscrossing the sky about two thousand yards in front of them. Another rig was visible in the distance.

"This is like a dream," Lela said, shaken by the sight. "I have had my head stuck in too many law books when this is what I should have been worrying about."

"Then you won't want to go any farther south," Russ warned. "It's even more of a mess down there. But there's nothin' out of compliance here. The oil companies are workin' right where they're supposed to be."

"It'll be okay, Lela. They'll tap the oil and gas reserves here and, eventually, they'll be gone."

"Kay, the well bores will stay in the ground. They will come back to redrill. It happens often now to recover reserves that have been bypassed."

"I know, I know," Kay conceded. "They could be here for a long time."

"Can I help you people with something?" a voice asked. The three of them turned from the view of the rig to find a short, stocky man dressed in a heavy blue parka and hard hat. His brown eyes studied them hard and then he said, "Oh, it's you, Bend. I didn't know you'd be back today. Sorry."

"Hey, Mike," Russ said, extending his hand. "This is Kay Westmore and Lela Newlin. They're also from the Interior office. Kay and Lela, this is Mike Johnson. He's the site manager here."

"Pleasure meeting you. Bend has already had a tour of the site and has been trailing around after me for the last two weeks."

"Hey, I've been on my best behavior," Russ protested.

Johnson started to laugh. "Yes you have, and it's been a pleasure working with you, Russ. And now I'd be more than happy to show you ladies around. Interested?" Johnson asked politely.

Kay nodded affirmatively, and she and Lela followed Johnson closer to the giant drilling rig. The shadow of the structure cut through the landscape and into the sky like a NASA rocket.

"This is a mobile drilling rig," Johnson explained. "That means we can move it from one place to another and cause less disruption to the land. It's a hundred and sixty feet high and cost about fifteen million to build." As they approached the rig, Johnson opened a door and they stepped inside an enclosure constructed to protect workers from frigid temperatures and high winds. Johnson flipped on the lights and simultaneously they all looked up, following the smooth cylindrical bore until it vanished into the base of the platform high above. "We're not quite ready to drill yet. But we should be underway next week. When that happens, the rig will actually house twenty-two workers. They'll operate the rig on two twelve-hour shifts each day."

"How many feet of exploratory drilling did you do in this area?" Kay asked.

Johnson quickly scanned his notes. "About a thousand feet. More than we had planned. Mostly due to poor weather conditions and faulty hydrocarbon readings."

"Do you have a map of the exploratory drilling sites?" Kay asked.

"Yes. I'll make sure you get that information."

"Listen, while we're in here and we can talk, I wanted to give you a message," Kay said. "Some of our equipment has been damaged while we've been working this area. Surveying reports have disappeared. Surveying markers have been moved or stolen, and the guys from the EPA have been hassled. I was hoping we could work out an end to this sort of thing. So far, to be quite honest, you guys are doing exactly what you're supposed to be doing. This kind of nonsense is only delaying a positive report being filed with the Department of the Interior."

"Russ talked to me about this last week," Johnson replied. "I did talk to my men, and I thought we had everything squared away."

"Can you talk to them again?" Kay asked.

"Yes, of course. Listen, we don't want any trouble with Interior. We worked too damned hard to get these leases."

"I understand," Kay agreed. "And we just want to complete our reports and get out of your way."

Johnson completed the tour and Kay, Russ, and Lela returned to their snowmobiles, still nestled near a group of evergreen trees away from the traffic and roar of heavy equipment. Russ took one look at the snowmobiles and yelled, "Where's Allen?"

Kay watched with growing anger as gasoline from the snowmobile's punctured gas tanks spilled onto the snow. "Unbelievable! Yes, where is Mr. Allen? He said he was going to be down here today."

Johnson pointed toward one of the outbuildings. "I saw him go toward the mess building about an hour ago. Say, I don't think my men did this. As you can see, we've got a skeleton crew on today, and those guys are busy working the equipment. I gave most of the crew some time off so we can start drilling next week. There won't be much rest after that."

"Not to worry, Mike," Kay said. "I believe this is another problem altogether."

Ten minutes later, Allen was skulking behind Russ toward the snowmobiles. "I found him at the mess all right. But he'd only been in there about fifteen minutes according to most of the workers."

Allen glanced at the leaking snowmobiles. "Hey, don't try pinning this on me. I've been busy reviewing the final surveying reports."

"Really?" Kay asked. "And where have you been doing that?"

"Like I told Bend, I've been in the mess for about two hours."

"Then you must be the invisible man," Russ countered. " 'Cause no one saw you in there until about fifteen minutes ago."

"Listen, this is a setup. I don't know anything about this," Allen insisted.

Russ scanned the immediate area. "Where's your snowmobile, Allen?"

"In back of the mess."

"Good. You won't be using it anymore today. It's gonna take Lela and Kay back to Anakruak."

Allen threw up his arms. "And how the hell am I supposed to get back?"

"You can walk, asshole." Russ nodded his head toward the

mess. "Let's check out Allen's snowmobile and then grab a cup of coffee. Afterward, you ladies can head back. I'll talk to Mike about hitching a ride. He's got some crews staying up near Anakruak."

"Good, I'll talk to Mike too. I'm sure he can get me a ride back," Allen said smugly. "I'll probably get first dibs over you, Bend."

"Don't count on it, buster."

Later that evening, Kay and Lela watched with great interest as Russ strode through the door into the smoky bar in Anakruak. "Where's Allen?" Kay asked as nonchalantly as possible.

"Hell, he's still trying to find a ride back. Seems no one at the drill site likes him any better than we do. They're pretty convinced that he's the one who's been causin' all the trouble and then blamin' it on the workers. Junior may have a long walk ahead of him."

"I think that calls for a celebratory drink," Kay said. "I'll even buy."

Chapter Six

Monday, ten days after their trip began, Dawn and Michelle from the EPA were on their way back to Barrow to conclude testing on the water samples and finalize their reports. The plans for that first week in February were for Russ and his EPA crew to continue surveying along the eastern shore of Lake Teshekpuk. Lela and Kay were headed to the western shore of the lake to check out an abandoned oil company site, which consisted of two outbuildings the townspeople of Anakruak claimed were filled with chemicals and built in an unleased area.

As she guided the snowmobiles in the direction of the abandoned site, Kay pressed the light on her compass watch. They were still heading southwest. Weather conditions had deteriorated in the last fifteen minutes, and the wind was so brutal it was kicking up a constant spray of snow. Kay had abandoned plans to follow the winter trail. In the darkness and blinding snow the trail was obliterated. From the glow of the lights behind her, Kay was able to monitor Lela's progress. The last thing she wanted to do was lose sight of her.

Lela and Kay had not spoken about the kiss since it happened three days before. There was an uncomfortable silence between them now that Kay hated. She chastised herself for crossing the line that always changed everything and hoped they could still be friends.

In the middle of her thoughts, the trees suddenly disappeared and the land dropped off into air. Kay felt herself in a free fall, the snowmobile no longer beneath her. She hit the ground with a thud and rolled into the blackness until she stopped face up, looking toward the sky. Blinking a few times, she tried to take stock of the situation. Her helmet had probably saved her life. Cautiously, she stretched her hands and her arms. Then she moved her legs. A sharp pain from her left ankle shot up her leg, and she bit her lip. Broken? She wasn't sure.

Kay sat up. The snowmobile had tumbled out of sight. Where was Lela, she thought. My God, did she fall, too? Turning over, Kay was able to prop herself up on her knees.

"Lela! Lela! Are you here?"

"Kay! Where are you?"

The voice came from above. Lela was still at the top of the culvert. "I'm about halfway down the culvert. It's pretty steep. I've hurt my ankle, but I think I'm okay."

"I will be there in a few minutes. Do not move!"

A few minutes seemed like an hour, but Kay realized Lela must be having problems getting to her. Up above, the culvert was almost a cliff face — the reason Kay had been sent hurtling into the icy air. That steep drop, along with the speed of the snowmobile, had created the momentum that carried her some distance before she hit the ground. She was lucky that the snow was soft here — new-fallen in the last couple of days.

Suddenly, Kay saw a flash in the darkness. It was Lela tied to a rope and carrying a handheld flashlight.

"Kay, are you all right?"

"I'm fine. Just cold. I can walk, no problem."

"Are you sure? That may not be a good idea."

"Hell, I've been in worse scrapes than this. I think it's just a sprain."

Lela stooped beside her. She touched the fabric of Kay's face mask with her hand. "I do not think you should try to walk. We need to get you back up that hill."

"And just how do you figure on managing that if I don't try to walk?" Kay snapped.

Lela smiled, put her hands on her hips, and shook her head. "Your stubbornness shows again, Kay. The slope is not as steep farther south. It is a gradual incline, and I can pull you up on this tarp."

"No way. I can hobble up that hill just as well as you can." Kay struggled until she was standing, weight on her good leg.

"Must you always be so difficult?"

"Is that what I'm being?"

"Yes."

"And you're not being stubborn, insisting on dragging me up the hill on a tarp?"

"I am trying to be helpful."

Kay peered at the southern slope. She was weary of the darkness. Of trying to work where she could not see. "Okay, what's the plan?"

"Fortunately, my snowmobile is fine. When I saw your headlights disappear over the cliff, I slammed on my brakes. It is lucky that I was far enough behind or we both would have gone sailing."

"Are you saying that's it's good you're pokey?"

"Maybe better to say that I am cautious."

"Okay, I can live with that."

"We will take my snowmobile to our original destination. I believe the old work site is not far from here. It will be good shelter for the night. We simply got off course due to the weather. But it has calmed somewhat in the last hour."

"You're the boss now."

"Kay, please sit down."

Kay did as she was told. She was beginning to believe there was a bit more dyke in Lela than she had ever thought possible. "Don't let me get in the way or anything."

"I am going to ignore this verbal sparring. Clearly, we have both been out in the cold too long." Lela went to work, folding the tarp and then sliding it underneath Kay. "Once, I had to do this for Robert, and he proved just as ornery." Threading a rope through some grommets at the top of the tarp, she finished the makeshift sled. Then Lela dragged Kay across the cold rutted ground for an eternity. Finally, Lela collapsed in the snow next to the snowmobile.

"Excuse me, Kay. I must rest for a moment."

"I should have walked."

"It matters little now. From here on in, we both ride."

Another forty-five minutes passed before Lela was able to find the old work site. It was located in the exact spot Kay had plotted on the map, but Lela had been correct. The weather had taken them slightly off course. Lela parked the snowmobile outside two empty wooden buildings. They were both in poor condition. One was more like a large shed. The second building, which was in slightly better shape, was about the size of two tennis courts. Kay guessed it had been used to store larger earthmoving equipment. Estimating the buildings to be about six months old, Kay hobbled around the perimeter. The buildings had been constructed using the cheapest possible material, mostly fiberboard and tin. They weren't meant to last long, only as long as the oil crews worked in that area.

Lela put her arm around Kay's waist and helped her inside. Propping Kay up in a corner, she headed back to the snowmobile for more supplies. About a half-hour later, Lela had a two-man tent set up inside the larger of the two buildings. There was only one sleeping bag, but Lela was unconcerned.

"I can sleep rolled up in the tarp. When Robert and I went on caribou and bear hunts, I slept on caribou skins or pine branches. I can sleep anywhere."

A small propane heater warmed the tent. Kay was relieved that the heater had been stowed on Lela's snowmobile instead of hers. For the first time that day, Kay threw her Polartec mask and gloves aside. "God, that heater feels good."

"It does. Now if only we had a bottle of wine."

"You mean you didn't bring one?"

"No. It was not on Russ's list."

"Speaking of Russ, he'll be expecting us at the airstrip in about an hour. We should try to raise him on the walkie-talkie. Tell him we're not going to make it."

Lela opened the tent flap. "I will try. Be back in a few minutes."

Kay rolled up her pants and checked her ankle. It was slightly bruised and swollen but nothing too serious. All in all, she had been extremely lucky not to have been killed sailing over that cliff. Suddenly, she felt not only relieved, but also hungry. She wondered if any food had been stashed on Lela's snowmobile.

Lela crawled back into the tent toting another small backpack. "I could not reach Russ. Too much static. It is snowing again, and the wind has picked up. We cannot go anywhere for some time, I am afraid."

"Great. At least tell me there's food in that sack."

"Yes. There is food in this sack. And a small Bunsen burner. Russ was very clear in his instructions about making sure that certain survival items were packed on everyone's snowmobile."

"Russ is a lifesaver."

Kay lay on her back and closed her eyes. She was tired. The snow, the tent, the whole incredible day reminded Kay of three years ago. Another storm. Another crisis, only that time it was with Grace Perry and they were at Wiseman near the Alaskan pipeline. She and Grace had spent the night in a ranger cabin. The next day they set out to Dietrich Camp, continuing with the pipeline inspection along the way. Unfortunately, they ran headlong into a terrible storm.

The cold had been biting, penetrating every protective layer. Kay had never been that cold before. The frigid air hovered like death, and for the first time she was afraid of the elements. Truly afraid.

Behind her Grace was yelling, "Kay, we've got to keep going. Do you hear me? Keep going, or we're going to freeze to death!"

No, that wasn't right. If they kept going they'd definitely freeze to death. They had to find shelter. Kay focused on the road ahead. They were still too far from the northern ranger cabin to make it. And they certainly weren't going to make it to Dietrich Camp. Up ahead she spotted a grove of pines to the east. She swerved the snowmobile toward them. They would have to construct their own shelter or they would both die.

"Kay, what are you doing? Damn it! You keep going, do you hear me?"

Grace's face was buried in Kay's back. Kay could barely

hear her through the headset. Disoriented and weak, they were both suffering from the early stages of hypothermia.

"I'm trying to save our lives, Grace. We're in big trouble here."

"Get this damned machine back on the road, Kay. That's a fucking order!"

"Shut up, Grace. For once, just shut up!"

Kay stopped the snowmobile in the middle of the pine grove where she saw a depression in the snow. She ordered Grace to sit on a blanket near the snowmobile's engine for temporary warmth, then she went to work.

With a collapsible shovel she dug out the depression within the circle of pines, clearing away the new-fallen snow. Underneath the new snow there was a layer of ice, which she cut into blocks with a sharp knife. She used the ice blocks to reinforce the trench walls. In the depression she set up the tent; it was recessed into the ground for added protection. Over the tent she anchored a plastic tarp to serve as a double windbreak. By the time she finished, she had to carry Grace inside. She had passed out and was moaning soft, inaudible words.

Kay got the last of the supplies she needed, then shut herself inside with Grace. She lit the small portable stove that ran on white gas. It would radiate some heat. She also lit the lantern that would provide light for up to thirteen hours. It, too, would give off a tiny amount of heat.

Unrolling both sleeping bags, Kay placed one inside the other for double insulation. She took off Grace's wet clothes, boots, socks. She replaced the damp socks with two pairs of dry ones and slid the woman, dressed only in thermal underwear, into the double sleeping bag. Ten minutes later, she made some tea. She coaxed Grace into consciousness and made her drink a few sips at a time.

"Where are we?" Grace asked weakly.

"In a hole in the ground."

113

Grace looked at Kay and started to laugh. "Are we dead then?"

"Not yet."

"Kay, would you like some soup?"

"Huh? What?" Kay sat up, startled.

Lela handed her a hot tin of soup. "You were deep in thought. But you are still hungry, no doubt."

"Yes, I am. Sorry. I was thinking about the trip along the pipeline three years ago. Grace and I got caught in a terrible storm on our way to Dietrich Camp. I honestly didn't think we'd make it."

"I am sure you knew just how to handle the situation."

"Well, the best part was that I didn't drive our snowmobile over a cliff. That helped."

Lela started to laugh. "Grace would not have been happy."

"Are you kidding? She would have fired me for that one."

"How is your ankle?"

"Actually, not bad at all. I was lucky. Just a slight sprain. Not even much swelling."

"Good." Lela sat on the tarp Indian-style. "Kay, have you thought any more about us?"

"I haven't been thinking about much else."

"Are we going to ignore what we feel?"

"What I did was extremely inappropriate."

"Maybe. But I am glad because I do have feelings for you, Kay."

"You do?"

"Yes. You are so much like —"

"Robert? But is that good?"

"And so much unlike him."

Kay shrugged. "I don't understand."

"It was the way I felt when I was near him. The same way I feel now with you. And you have brought laughter back into

114

my life — you and your stubbornness." Lela laughed and slid her hand across Kay's cheek.

Kay threw the soup tin aside. She wasn't hungry for food, and she was tired of the inner debate she was having with herself. About losing Stef, about being hurt again. Reaching for Lela's hand, Kay pulled her closer, wrapping her arms around her shoulders. "I'm sorry. I guess I'm the one who's confused. I just lost Stef, and I don't want to experience that torment again anytime soon."

"I understand that you have been hurt. But I cannot help what I feel, Kay. I cannot begin to explain it except to say that I feel alive for the first time in seven years."

In the dim glow of a white-gas lantern, Kay gazed into Lela's smoky gray eyes, running her hand alongside the soft skin of Lela's cheek. Lela's eyes searched Kay's and found something. Kay could feel Lela touching her somewhere deep inside, and a chill passed up and down her spine. Leaning into a kiss that was soft and warm and then suddenly hot with passion, Kay felt her cheeks flush and her thighs burn. Lela wriggled out of her jacket, and Kay reached down to unbutton Lela's shirt. Her bra was satin and lace, its white color a contrast to the sepia-toned skin. Kay's fingers slid easily over hard nipples. Unsnapping the garment, Kay threw it aside.

Lela's caramel skin was fragrant with a delicate aroma of summer flowers. Her nipples, large and dark like exotic fruit, responded to her touch. In her mouth they grew harder and more sensitive. Lela's moans echoed through the tent and into the crevices of the building that surrounded them. Kay drew each nipple into her mouth, caressing them with her tongue. At the same time, Kay unzipped Lela's jeans, sliding her hand between warm thighs.

Squirming out of her jeans, Lela opened herself to Kay, who slid down Lela's stomach leaving soft kisses every inch of the way. She made love to Lela with her tongue, her passion overflowing with every stroke and cry from Lela's heart. No words passed between them, only movements and breaths and moans and pleasure. When Lela climaxed, Kay's heart fluttered with joy. She smiled, laughed, and then rose to kiss Lela, filling her mouth with the passion that still remained.

Lela rolled on top of Kay and straddled her stomach. Tracing the softness of Kay's lips with her tongue, Lela took Kay's hand and slipped it between her thighs. "I want you inside me, Kay."

The soft mound of Lela's hair was wet against Kay's fingers. Stroking Lela as she moved, Kay followed the rhythm of Lela's hips as she pushed herself to orgasm. Grabbing Lela's baby-soft skin with her free hand, Kay pulled Lela into each thrust. The moments were a blur of curves, hot skin, and thrashing hips.

"Kay, you fill the emptiness inside with so much love."

"I do love you, Lela."

As she arched her back and shuddered, Lela held Kay inside of her. Sighing deeply, Lela whispered, "It is you, Kay. You fill me with so much passion."

The evening swirled around Kay's head with Lela's touches and the oneness they shared long into the night. In Kay's mind, nothing was scripted. Their passion was spontaneous, their feelings raw and exposed. Lela curled in a ball against Kay and breathed softly into Kay's chest. Closing her eyes, Kay held on to Lela as tightly as she could.

"Tell me more about Robert," Kay whispered.

"Why?"

"Because then I'll know more about you."

Lela brushed her fingernails along Kay's forearm. "He was physically strong, and tall like you. He once dragged a bear through the snow for over a mile. But inside he was gentle, also like you. Like a light wind brushing over the snow. The other villagers respected him for his honesty and good humor. But he could also be quiet, contemplative. He liked to sip whiskey by the fire and watch me while I sewed caribou skins."

"I like watching you too."

~ ~ ~ ~ ~

The next morning Kay turned over into Lela's arms. It was odd to find someone other than Stef beside her. As Lela continued to sleep, Kay kissed her forehead, her thoughts drifting back to the night before. The intensity of their love-making had shocked Kay. Lela was passionate, exciting, erotic to the depths of her spirit — a spirit Kay felt she had touched. This calm, uncomplicated, and down-to-earth woman had unleashed another side to herself that stole Kay's breath away. Kay had let go too, something she had always been able to do over time. But not in one night. Not like that.

Lela stirred and opened her eyes. Their smoky hue was like an early morning mist that enveloped Kay. Lela smiled and cupped Kay's face with her hands. "Good morning, darling. I have missed you."

Kissing Lela's fingertips, Kay felt a pang of fear. It was the same fear that had been gnawing at her all morning. What would happen when she returned to Fairbanks? She would be alone again — something she expected and had resolved to live with, at least for a while. But Lela had changed those expectations, and that frightened her. A string of disastrous relationships preyed on her mind. Would this be another? In an instant, the inner debate began again — and the fear of losing Lela was all she could think about. Willingly, she tried to shut down her emotions. "Lela, we need to talk. Right here. Right now."

"I want to kiss you first."

Lela's fingertips wandered through Kay's hair, making her scalp tingle. Warm against Kay's, Lela's mouth was gentle but insistent. Kay wanted to drown herself in that moment and forget about the rest of the world, even if it meant staying in that frozen Arctic wilderness forever. She closed her eyes and massaged Lela's shoulders, then pulled away. "Lela, we have to talk."

"What is it, Kay? You are upset."

"Concerned."

"Tell me."

"I do care for you, Lela. But what's happening here frightens me. I'm not very good at explaining stuff like this. But I want to be honest with you."

"You are afraid because of Stef?"

"I'm afraid because of me. I've never been very successful in relationships. I've made a lot of mistakes that I don't want to repeat. I don't want to be hurt, and I don't want to hurt you."

Lela buried her head in Kay's shoulder. "I would never hurt you, Kay."

"I've heard those words before."

"Not from me."

"Lela, I'm going back to Fairbanks. Your life is in Barrow with your people. I'm thinking about that too. How on earth can this possibly work?"

"How does love ever work? There is no obstacle too great. Do you not love me, Kay?" Lela looked up at Kay, her eyes filling with tears. "Is that what you are trying to say?"

"I'm saying that I'm afraid, and that's a hard thing for me to admit. I'm not sure I know how to love anyone right now or that I've ever known how. I mean, I seem to keep screwing it up."

"You knew how to love me last night. I felt you touch my heart, Kay. For seven years I have waited to feel like that again."

"You've had no lovers since Robert?"

"There have been a few. But none that lasted."

"Men?"

"Actually, there have been three, and they have all been women. Do you want to hear about each one of them?"

"Why didn't the relationships last?"

"As I said, for seven years I have waited to feel like this again."

"And I've waited a lifetime to even begin to get it right."

118

"No more of this talk. Make love to me again, Kay. I want to come in your arms with you inside me."

Kay lowered her voice to a whisper. "I love you, Lela." She stared at the dark eyebrows and full lips. Teasingly, she bit Lela's lower lip, then kissed her mouth quickly, then deeply, her hand running through Lela's hair and over the small of her back. Lela threw the outer layer of the sleeping bag aside and pulled Kay on top of her. Kay kissed Lela's neck, her mouth melting into the warm, supple skin. Lela nibbled softly on Kay's ear, causing the hair on Kay's neck to stand on end. Sliding her tongue over Lela's nipples, she listened to the soft moans, felt Lela's body rubbing against her thigh. She kissed Lela's stomach, parted her thighs and slipped inside. Bracing her wrist with her other hand, Kay slowly fucked Lela, following the urges of Lela's body. Lela grabbed Kay's shoulders and wrapped her legs around Kay's back. She continued to thrust her hips, urging Kay deeper inside. Then Kay felt a shudder and heard Lela gasp, "Kay, my darling. Feel me coming." Lela's muscles tightened over Kay's hand, and her body arched forward with a deep, satisfying moan. Kay kissed the inside of Lela's thighs, her tongue tasting the salt of their passion.

"Such orgasms you give me, Kay."

"I'm enjoying them as much as you."

"They are from us. Our love makes them strong. It is everything I feel for you pulsating through me. You make me feel so beautiful."

"You are beautiful, Lela. My Arctic princess."

"And you, my darling Kay, are the dyke of my dreams."

Kay laughed so hard, she gasped for breath. Then she took a deep breath and made love to Lela again.

Later that morning, Kay stood just outside the oil consortium shacks. Her ankle felt better, and she had only a

119

slight limp. The storm had continued through the night, and the snow was still heavy. The snowmobile was covered under a mound of the white stuff, and the one thing they didn't have was a shovel. Luckily, the oil company crews had left some shovels behind. Rusted and pitted, they would still do the job.

Lela kissed Kay's cheek. The old shovels creaked with the weight of the snow as they began to dig out the snowmobile. Thirty minutes later, Kay cranked up the machine and maneuvered it into the smaller outbuilding. Clearing some frost from the gas gauge with her fingers, Kay noted that there was a half tank left — just enough to get them back to the airstrip if they were lucky. Kay studied the sky. The dark cloud cover worried her. They were storm clouds. "We won't be going anywhere today. Not in this."

"You are right, Kay. The sky is thick with clouds. Perhaps tomorrow it will clear."

"Let's hope so. If it'll at least quit snowing, we can make it back to the airfield."

"Yes, I think we can too."

"In the meantime, we may as well do some work." Kay scanned the small shack with a flashlight. "Let's inventory these buildings. Also take some photos. This work area's definitely in a restricted zone."

"There are also some drums out back. I do not know what they contain."

"We'll take some photos, then try to get some samples. That stuff could be anything."

An hour later, Kay had a complete inventory of everything contained inside the two buildings. In addition to finding two well bores that indicated illegal drilling in the area, they were also keeping company with some highly dangerous substances. The most dangerous of these was benzene, which was on the

Environmental Protection Agency's list of the top twenty most dangerous chemicals.

"That's what the drums are out back," Kay explained, finishing up her notes. "Twenty-three drums of benzene. The drums look fairly new, so they haven't been out here too long. Why they were dumped here, I don't know. It's not a chemical associated with petroleum drilling. Used mostly to make rubber and dyes. Benzene is used to make petroleum products, but not for extracting oil from the ground. That's why I'm puzzled."

"Then why would the oil companies have such a dangerous chemical here?"

"They wouldn't. All this equipment is old. Like the shovels we found. The benzene containers are new. This entire area will have to be cleaned up. There's one thing that really bothers me, though. About this benzene."

"What?"

Kay bit down on the end of her pencil. "Remember when Dawn and Michelle were taking water samples from the lake?"

"Yes, of course."

"Michelle talked about that job they were doing at the Gates of the Arctic. That some crazy environmental terrorist had threatened to poison the area with benzene."

"You are right, Kay. She did mention that."

"I think there must be a connection."

"That is an evil thought."

"Think about it, Lela. How important is this area to your people's survival?"

"It is critical."

"Then it's also a good target for a group that wants to make a political statement and do a lot of environmental damage at the same time."

"I hope what you are thinking is not true."

"So do I."

~ ~ ~ ~ ~

The snow stopped early Wednesday morning. Kay wandered outside just before five and stood in the darkness listening to the quiet. The stillness broke with the *whoosh* of helicopter blades. Hovering in a clearing about a thousand yards from where Kay stood, the military helicopter settled into the snow. The main door opened and Russ stepped out, the burly figure of him unmistakable against the lights of the helicopter. Kay strapped on her snowshoes and lumbered like Big Foot to the edge of the woods. She waved her arms and her flashlight, and Russ waved back. Minutes later, he was standing in front of her, huffing and puffing a cloud of white vapor into the crackling air.

"Kay, you have a way of always worryin' me. Don't you think you've given me enough gray hairs?"

"Apparently not."

Russ wrapped his arms completely around her. "Good to see you, boss. Lela okay, too?"

"Yes. I think she's still sleeping."

"Let's get you both back to Anakruak. Couple of days of rest are in order."

"We're fine, really. A good hot meal would be nice."

"No problem."

"Russ, before we go I need you to look at something for me."

"Sure, boss."

Kay led Russ around to the west side of the building. "What's your reaction to this?"

Kay steadied her flashlight as Russ stooped down, brushing some of the new snow from the lime-green barrels. "Damn, Kay. This is dangerous stuff. How'd it get here?"

"Good question. Lela and I took photos of everything. Samples, too. There's no reason for this stuff to be here. The oil companies wouldn't be using it for anything. At least nothing I can think of."

"You're right. There's somethin' crummy about this.

Somethin' that just don't add up. We'll be reportin' it, of course."

"It's the first thing we'll report to Grace. Personally and confidentially." Kay's temples were throbbing, and her throat was dry. "Russ, here's the other thing."

"What?"

"This isn't the first dump of benzene that's been found."

"What?"

"Days ago at Teshekpuk Lake, Dawn and Michelle talked about a dump of benzene that had been found a month ago at the Gates of the Arctic Preserve. The EPA believed it was an isolated incident."

"Not any more."

"No, not any more."

"Damn, Kay. We do have a way of stumblin' right smack into things. Full force."

Chapter Seven

After their two-day stay in the rundown oil company shacks, the cabin in Anakruak felt like the Taj Mahal to Lela and Kay. Allen and Russ were still living down the street, keeping an uneasy peace now that the EPA team had gone back to Barrow.

"Yeah, it's just me and Toadhead now. I'm tryin' to be nice to him, Kay. But it ain't easy."

"How is Mr. Allen anyway?"

"Smug as ever. We didn't find anything, Kay. Surveyed up and down the lease area south of the lake. The oil companies are workin' right where they're supposed to be. I should know. Allen's been remindin' me about it every damn day. The guy's a total wiener."

"And he has his own survey and testing results that match ours?"

"Yep. Right down to the last meter and water pH."

Kay sat on a wooden stool near the fire. "I'm glad, Russ. Grace will be relieved. That old oil company camp's not enough to hang the oil companies."

"The benzene dump is."

"The oil companies don't have anything to do with that. I'd bet my life on it."

"You call Grace yet?"

"I can't get through. I'll try again first thing in the morning."

"Kay and Russ. We are having a celebration down the street. Real food. Not freeze-dried and not out of a can." Lela pulled Kay from the stool. "The bartender has promised not to shoot. Everyone will behave."

Kay grabbed her coat. "No shooting? I think I'm disappointed. It won't be the same neighborhood bar we know and love."

"Where's Allen?" Russ asked with a grimace.

"I am afraid he is already at the bar drinking," Lela said, helping Kay with her coat.

Pulling on her gloves, Kay said, "We'll do what we normally do when Mr. Allen is present. Annoy or ignore him."

Russ opened the door. "Annoying him is much more fun."

Allen was sitting at the bar, fist wrapped around a beer mug, watching the crowd of locals with obvious disdain. The sneer on his face said it all. "Look who we have here. Now the gathering is complete." Allen swigged his beer. His face was unshaven, his clothes rumpled. "I just knew I couldn't make it through the evening without you three."

"We feel the same way," Kay said, looking him up and

down. "What the hell happened to you, Allen? You run out of clothing or what?"

"No. I just figured if you're going to be among the locals, you might as well look and smell the part."

"Don't start, buster," Russ threatened. "I've had just about as much from you as I'm gonna take. C'mon, Kay, Lela. There's a small table over there. Only room enough for three." Russ pulled Kay by the arm. "Quick, before I hafta hurt the guy."

"Ta ta," Allen said with a wave. "Try the whale-blubber appetizer. I hear it's just fabulous."

"He's drunk again," Kay said with disgust. "The consortium needs to pull the plug on that guy."

"Yeah, even the oil companies can do better than that," Russ agreed. "I don't think he's taken a shower in about three days."

"Actually, the whale blubber is quite good." Lela draped her parka over a chair. "They coat it in a bread mixture and deep-fry it. It is considered a delicacy."

Russ squirmed and glanced at the menu written on a chalkboard over the bar. "Snails are considered a delicacy too. But I haven't tried them yet. I think I'll go for the salmon burger again. And some real fried potatoes."

The Inupiat villagers were out in full force. They sang songs in Inupiaq about the caribou, the whale, and the spirits of the land. The singing was more like chanting, the music mostly percussion. The dancing was festive with high steps and sweeping arm movements. Kay was trying to take it all in when Lela pulled her to her feet.

"Come. I will teach you the proper steps."

"No way. I can't even do regular dancing."

"You will learn. I am a good teacher."

Kay watched Lela and tried to copy her steps. But, as

usual, she felt like she had two left feet. "Lela, I'm making a fool of myself."

"You are not. You look beautiful, and you are a good dancer."

"I'll accept the compliment just to make myself feel better. The real truth is that I don't know what the hell I'm doing. What is this dance anyway?"

"It is called Happy Travel. We have had a hard trip but have come back safe."

Kay watched as Lela held her arms at either side, palms down, rising above and below her waistline alternately. Both hands floated into the air as her feet stepped left and then right, her neck and shoulders moving with the beat of the music. "The dance suits you. I like the way you move — on and off the dance floor."

"I respond to you, Kay."

"Too bad I can't kiss you right now. Or hold you close."

"Later you can hold me close and kiss me. I hope again and again."

Lela tugged playfully until Kay fell into a heap across the mattress. The mattress was in the corner room of the small house where Dawn had slept. Lela had covered it with caribou skins she found in the loft. The somewhat stiff animal hair scratched Kay's face.

"Man, I really can't do this."

"Do what?" Lela asked, nibbling on Kay's ear.

"Make love on these animal skins. They're itchy."

Lela burst out laughing. "You have been spoiled by goose-feather sleeping bags."

"Maybe. But that's an animal I can deal with."

"Yes, darling." Lela returned with their sleeping bags and spread them across the animal hides. "There. I do not mind pampering you. Nothing but goose feathers for you, my love."

Grasping Lela's hand, Kay kissed the tip of each finger. "I'm lucky to have you in my life."

"I am the lucky one. To have had one great love — and now another in the same lifetime. Many people never find it once."

"Or wait forty years to find it." Kay rolled over on top of Lela. She kissed Lela's forehead, her cheeks, and her chin. Teasingly, she ran her tongue along the outside of Lela's ear.

"Kay, you are driving me crazy."

"I hope so." Holding Lela close, Kay buried her face in Lela's neck. She kissed the soft curves and listened as Lela's breaths grew quick and her body went limp in Kay's arms.

"Kiss me, Kay."

"I was getting to the kiss, honest. It's just that you're so sexy and I want to take you in slowly. Like a Van Gogh painting. All the impressions."

"Have I impressed you so far?"

"Absolutely." As Kay stripped Lela's shirt off, she kissed her deeply. The silky black bra was soft against Kay's lips, Lela's skin even softer. She rubbed the palms of her hands over Lela's breasts and caressed two luscious nipples.

Unsnapping the bra, Lela threw it aside. "Don't ever stop loving me, Kay."

"Not a chance." Kay made love to Lela, touching every inch of her with kisses and caresses. As she listened to Lela's soft moans and felt Lela's body quiver with multiple orgasms, Kay suddenly felt tears streaming down her face.

"Kay, darling, why are you crying?"

"Because you give me such joy."

"I am glad. And I am not finished yet." Tugging at Kay's sweatshirt, Lela pulled it over her head. Kay closed her eyes and sighed as Lela ran her tongue across Kay's nipples. "I love you, Kay."

Kay felt a swing of emotions as Lela made love to her. She lost herself in the gentle touch of the woman who had become her lover. Nothing else mattered except the sensation of Lela's breath against her cheek. Nothing else mattered but the force of Lela's tongue pushing her slowly to the edge. As the orgasm cut through the center of her, she closed her eyes and slowly ran her fingers through Lela's hair. The touch of it was as supple and rich as the orgasm that coursed through her body. But as the orgasm faded she wondered if the commitment they shared would also fade. It had been that way in her world for so long. So many attempts at love and far too many good-byes.

Lela lay with her head on Kay's chest. "You are thinking so hard, Kay. What is it?"

"Loving you frightens me."

"There is not much I can do to ease your fears except be here tomorrow and the next day."

"I haven't had much success with love."

"That is the one great difference between us. It will take time, Kay. I have been given the task to heal a heart that has been broken more than once."

"You've already accomplished that task. I'm just worried about what we're going to do when I have to go back to Fairbanks. We haven't talked about that yet."

"There is plenty of time for talk. But not now."

Early Thursday morning, one day after being rescued from an Arctic blizzard, Kay sat and stewed. She almost wished she were back in the wilderness stranded alone with Lela. For more than ten minutes, she had been waiting for Grace to come to the phone. Last evening she had tried to reach Grace for almost two hours with no luck. The cell phone signal had kept breaking up, and now the phone buzzed annoyingly in her ear. Kay passed the time by studying her notes from the last two weeks. It was the benzene that glared back at her.

Benzene in the Alaska wilderness. In the Gates of the Arctic and near Teshekpuk Lake. Barrels buried in the snow and hidden behind work buildings. It could only mean one thing.

"Kay? Grace here. Have you been waiting long?"

"Ten minutes maybe."

"I'm sorry. I have a new administrative assistant. He's very adept in some areas. Getting messages to me promptly is not one of them."

Despite her mood, that comment made Kay smile. Grace was the real-life version of Murphy Brown when it came to administrative assistants. She went through them on a weekly basis. "Listen, I tried to get you last night for over two hours, but the signal wouldn't hold. I wanted to summarize my report to you over the phone before I sent it to Washington. You'll need to advise me on what information to make public at the meetings in Barrow next week. I'm not sure full disclosure is appropriate or wise."

"Why, Kay? What did you find?"

"Only one violation by the oil companies. An abandoned work site located well inside the restricted area. Two well bores left in the ground. They were drilling illegally. And it seems they planned to come back and redrill, if necessary."

"That won't happen. However, all in all, this one violation is nothing to be overly concerned about. In fact, if that's the only violation you found, I consider this great news."

"In that respect it is."

"What else did you find? Let me have it. I can tell it's bad."

"Benzene."

Grace didn't miss a beat. Clearly, she knew something about the benzene. "Where?"

"More than twenty barrels located at the abandoned oil-company site. The barrels aren't old. Haven't been there that long. Don't belong to the oil consortium either, I'm certain of that." There was silence at the other end of the line. "Grace?"

"That's an alarming report, Kay. One of our other teams found a similar cache of benzene just last month."

"In the Gates of the Arctic?"

"That's correct. But here's the other news. Another dump of benzene was found near Allakaket five days ago."

"Terrorism?"

"Possibly. But let's not discuss anything further over this open phone line. Make your full report to me immediately, Kay. Get it to me by Monday. Fly it here if you have to."

"You'll have it Monday."

As was typical with Grace, she risked nothing. First thing Monday morning, a military helicopter picked up Kay and Russ at Anakruak. The copter flew them to Barrow. From Barrow, a small plane flew them to Seattle. From Seattle a government jet flew them directly to Washington, D.C. Lela stayed in Anakruak to compile the results and data collected from all the teams that had been deployed into the reserve over the past three weeks.

A black stretch limousine with the presidential seal was waiting for Kay and Russ at the airport. The inside was completely high-tech with every convenience imaginable. Kay could have taken a nap comfortably in the spacious backseat. The urge to stretch across the soft leather interior was almost overwhelming. They hadn't had much rest in the last twelve hours.

Russ yawned and fumbled around, pushing buttons and opening compartments to keep himself amused. "You think the president actually rides in this thing?"

"It's a car from his fleet, so I imagine he does. Grace has probably ridden in this thing too."

"Yeah, she's got the life, I'm sure. Grace must really have some news to go snatchin' us outta the wilderness like that.

131

Man, I didn't even have a suit to wear. But I did pick my best pair of jeans."

Kay eyed Russ carefully. "The sport jacket helps. Look at me. Thank God I packed these khakis. But this denim shirt is hardly appropriate."

Simultaneously, they both looked down at their feet. They were wearing identical field boots — huge brown high-top hikers with rubber tips and soles. "Shit," Russ said. "We're a couple of first-rate dorks."

"My feet look like they're size twelve, for God's sake." Kay yanked at her khakis, trying to hide the massive boots.

"Once Grace gets a load of us, we may hafta walk back to Anakruak."

Kay and Russ felt even more self-conscious sitting in the plush waiting room outside Grace's office in the Department of the Interior building. Like every other government structure in Washington, the outside of the building was constructed of huge sand-colored cement blocks. Inside, however, the halls were thickly carpeted and the walls were decorated with expensive artwork. Security was tight, and both Russ and Kay were given the wand treatment twice before they were escorted to the waiting room. Grace's newest administrative assistant appeared downright terrorized when security personnel left them seated in the lounge.

"He's still staring at us," Kay whispered.

"No he ain't."

"He is so. Out of the corner of his eye."

"He's typin', for Pete's sake."

"Is not. He's been checking us out for the last ten minutes. Like we're going to whip out an Uzi or something and blast everyone in the building before heading to the White House to do the same."

"Listen, you couldn't get a safety pin through the security checks we just went through. I feel violated."

Suddenly the outside office door flew open. It was Grace. She was dressed in a precisely tailored black power suit with an ivory blouse and matching gold necklace and earrings. Kay thought she looked stunning, and felt even more like an oaf.

"Kay, Russ. Come in, please."

Kay and Russ plodded across the plush tan carpeting, rubber-soled boots squeaking in unison. Grace flashed a look of annoyance. "Don't you both look absolutely charming."

"Sorry, Grace. We had limited access to the proper clothing at such short notice." Kay sat down in a leather chair in front of Grace's desk and nearly disappeared. She straightened herself up and hung on to the arms of the chair to keep from sinking a second time. "Obviously, you needed us here immediately."

"Yes, of course."

When Grace sat down, Russ finally sat down too. "Good to see you, Grace."

"And you, Russ. I'd like to be civil and offer you something to eat and drink, but I might as well get right to the point. The way you're dressed matters little, and I didn't mean to infer that. It was just my attempt at some humor since you're here for a briefing on some very serious matters. You've both helped to unearth a potentially catastrophic situation we've been working on for the past month. You seem to have a knack for this sort of thing."

"What is it, Grace?" Russ asked, his hand finding his beard, stroking it intently. "Is this benzene thing even more widespread than what we've already found?"

"Yes, that's exactly right. Kay analyzed the situation correctly. You were absolutely on target, Kay, in assuming that there's a connection between the EPA's response to environmental terrorism threats last month and the benzene you found this month."

Kay nodded. "When Michelle and Dawn were at the Gates of the Arctic reserve they were looking for benzene. They mentioned it at Teshekpuk Lake."

"Yes, and then you and Lela found the benzene dump at the old Alyeska Consortium site. Five days before that, I got a call that benzene has been found near Allakaket." Grace grabbed a box and some file folders. "Both of you please come with me. I want to show you some slides I think you'll find particularly interesting."

Russ and Kay followed Grace down a long corridor and into a small amphitheater. Grace pressed some buttons, and a large motorized screen dropped from the wall at the same time the lights dimmed. Kay and Russ sat in the first row. From a laptop at the front console, Grace operated the electronic slides.

The first slide was of northern Alaska. "This orange circle here represents the dump of benzene the EPA team found in the Endicott Mountains in the Gates of the Arctic Preserve," Grace explained, highlighting the area with a laser pen. "That's the dump Dawn and Michelle mentioned to you."

As the second slide came up, Kay noticed it was the exact same map with another orange circle at Allakaket, a town south of the Gates of the Arctic. "This area represents a second dump of benzene found at Allakaket near the Kanuti National Wildlife Refuge." Grace again circled the area with the laser pen. "Third slide is another benzene dump found at Prudhoe Bay. Fourth slide, another dump found at Nuiqsut. Fifth slide represents the dump Kay found at Teshekpuk Lake. Sixth slide, a dump found just north of Point Lay on the coast this morning."

"All benzene dumps?" Russ asked.

"All benzene dumps. And here's the most interesting slide of all."

The last slide connected all the dumps with a horizontal and vertical line in the shape of a large T.

"As you can see, the dump sites intersect to form a large

T on the map. The vertical line of the T runs directly through the middle of the one hundred and fifty-four-degree and one hundred and fifty-two-degree parallels. The top of the T runs precisely along the seventy-degree parallel and cuts like a razor through the National Petroleum Reserve."

"Oh my God," Kay said aloud. "Environmental terrorism with a capital T."

"Yes, I'm sorry to confirm."

Russ shifted uncomfortably in his chair. "Well I'll be damned. There are more nuts than we can keep track of out there."

"We'll have to keep track of them or we'll have an environmental nightmare on our hands. Let me add that all of these dumps, except for the one found at the Gates of the Arctic, were discovered in the last two weeks. Kay's call confirmed what we've been thinking and fearing for the past two weeks — that there's a connection between the dumps. As a result, we believe there may be several more in the National Petroleum Reserve, and possibly one or two more between Howard Hill and Umiat."

The lights brightened and the screen disappeared into the ceiling. Kay felt numb and Russ looked shell-shocked.

"It's the government's belief that these benzene dumps were placed a few months ago with the intent to dump during the summer thaw." Grace sat down in the seat next to Kay. "But someone got cranky about a month ago and made some threats. That's the only reason we're on to them now. The only reason we sent an EPA team to the Gates of the Arctic."

Russ's head snapped up from a concentrated gaze. He continued to paw at his beard. "You're right about the summer, Grace. Store the stuff all winter and dump it when the water's moving. The damage would be freakin' unbelievable. Benzene takes awhile to dissolve in water. The stuff would travel up and down the rivers, linger in the lakes, and get into the ground. It would be everywhere."

135

Kay couldn't sit still any longer. "We have to get back, Grace. Right away."

"Kay, we're going to deploy fifteen to twenty teams in the reserve area. But no one knows this land like you, Russ, and Lela. We'll get you a complete set of briefing reports and maps from my office. I've already got you booked back to Seattle on a six o'clock flight."

"Thanks, Grace. We'll give you regular updates."

"Be careful. Whoever's planning on releasing this stuff into the ground or water is a bloody lunatic or the leader of a group of lunatics. They could be watching us. We don't know. And we don't know how much benzene is still out there."

Russ shook his head and shoved his hands into his pockets. "We've had experience with lunatics before. Let them watch. We'll get them anyway."

Chapter Eight

Just after midnight on Tuesday morning, Lela opened the door to the house in Anakruak. The news was written all over her face. One phone call from Grace had told her all she needed to know.

"Kay, we have a great deal of trouble here. I am afraid for my people." Lela slid her arms around Kay's shoulders and hugged her tightly.

"Don't worry. We'll find the benzene and the scumbags who put it out there. Teams have been deployed all along the seventy-degree parallel from Prudhoe Bay to north of Point Lay."

"It is unbelievable. In all this time I have worked for the government I have never even considered terrorism like this.

Bombs, guns, angry voices. I got used to thinking about these things. But chemicals that will destroy and kill and ruin the land — how could I ever believe such a thing possible?"

"Our teams will find the benzene. Then we'll trace the chemical production, the shipments. These people always leave a trail."

"I missed you, Kay."

"I missed you, too."

Thoughts of benzene and environmental terrorism were temporarily forgotten. Being in Lela's arms, Kay felt whole again. Meeting Lela had made her realize that a piece of her had always been missing. Even in Stef's arms she had not been whole, most certainly not in Barbara's. But in Lela's arms she became the person she knew she was and more. Because Lela had listened and connected to her heart, finally understanding the empty space inside of her.

"You must make peace with your sister, Kay," Lela had said one night out of the blue. "It is a source of great pain and emptiness for you."

"I want to, but I don't know how."

"You do not have to know how. You only have to recognize when the time is right. The time will come, and it will be up to you to accept that moment and find it in your heart to forgive."

"I love my sister."

"I know."

Lela did know. She had heard the pain in Kay's voice and had listened quietly as Kay talked about her sister, their constant disagreements, and their mutual disdain. Lela had heard the words of bitterness but had also felt the love as well as the struggle of two sisters to connect with one another, despite everything that had happened in the past. Lela did know — but then it seemed that Lela sensed and knew everything about Kay.

Accepting Lela into her arms, Kay caressed Lela's neck with soft, biting kisses. Lela smelled like spring lilacs, and her skin felt like soft petals against her face. Kay cupped the fullness of Lela's breasts, her knee rubbing firmly between Lela's thighs, eliciting soft moans and quick breaths. Kay sucked Lela's nipples until they were hard and swollen inside her mouth. Lela's fingernails crisscrossed and cut into Kay's back.

Opening herself to Kay, Lela's deep brown thighs glistened with excitement. "Fuck me, Kay. I have missed you inside me."

Finding the wetness between Lela's legs, Kay began with gentle thrusts until Lela's movements urged her deeper inside. Kay hand-fucked her slowly, then more forcefully until she felt Lela's muscles tightening. With final urgent thrusts, Lela arched her back and shuddered, a wave of orgasm pulsating against Kay's fingertips.

Kissing the perspiration from Lela's forehead, Kay gulped some air to calm her own breathing. "You exhaust me, Miss Newlin."

"Do I?"

"Yes. But it's an absolute pleasure. I wish all my exhaustion were this much fun."

"Then I will continue to exhaust you."

"Just love me, Lela."

"That is the one thing you do not have to worry about."

At the dawn of that same February morning there was a hint of light at the horizon. The daylight during their brief trip to Washington had thrown Kay off balance. She had finally grown accustomed to the darkness, but now the Arctic darkness was finally dissolving into soft shadows of sunlight that made the snow valleys gleam.

Kay was tired but wide-eyed. She had hardly slept at all. Her mind raced all night with thoughts about the benzene — thousands of barrels hidden throughout the reserve. And then she had tossed and turned with thoughts of Lela until she finally dozed for an hour or two. Still, the lack of sleep put her on edge.

Kay, Russ, and Lela ate breakfast in silence. The coffee tasted bitter to Kay and the eggs were too dry. Russ was fidgety too, stroking his beard and pouring over maps. Lela sat with her eyes closed, lost in thought. Wondering what they would find that day, Kay finally spoke in desperation, knowing that the time had come.

"We should get going. Are the snowmobiles ready?"

Russ's head snapped up and he quickly began to fold the maps he was studying. "I'll go check on them. They should be ready. I gassed them up last night."

"At two in the morning," Lela said. "I heard him."

Kay smiled. "Doesn't seem like anyone got much sleep last night."

"I will go with Russ. We will check on the snowmobiles."

"Thanks. I'll be out in a few minutes."

Kay sat with her head in her hands. The past month and a half had been exciting and frightening at the same time. But now what she loved most — the Alaskan wilderness — was being threatened with the worst kind of terrorism. This time it wasn't oil but something far more lethal. This time it wasn't an antiquated pipeline but an organized enemy they did not know. Kay got up and grabbed her pack. The sun had finally risen over the Alaskan tundra, but the day seemed just as dark as the day she arrived in Barrow.

"Westmore!" the voice yelled as Kay headed for the snowmobiles in a stupor. "Just what do you think you're doing?"

Kay swung around to find Allen inches from her face. He was making a mistake to cause trouble this morning. She wasn't in the mood. "What's your problem, Allen? Your job is over. I'd thought you'd be on your way back to Barrow by now."

"I'm sure you did. Mr. Bend gave me the whole story about

the end of this investigation. That there'd be some kind of report made about the findings in a couple of weeks. What I want to know is what happened to the meeting that was supposed to be this week? It's been canceled, I hear. Why? That's what I want to know. What are you waiting for?"

"It's been postponed, Allen. That's all I can tell you and all you need to know."

"Then what are you still doing here? What's this early morning trek you're going on? If the investigation is really over, shouldn't you be heading back to Fairbanks?"

Kay rubbed her eyes and tried to gather her wits. "Listen, Allen. I'm in a hurry here. An emergency has come up. The investigation of the oil companies is over. This is an entirely different matter. Quite frankly, it's confidential."

Allen folded his arms across his chest and kicked at the snow with the heel of his boot. "I don't believe a word you're telling me. You're up to something, Westmore. Why don't you face the fact that this time the government and the people of Alaska aren't going to succeed in railroading the oil companies?"

"Okay, that's it. It's time for *you* to listen." Kay's brain snapped. The pressure of the day ahead caused her to lose control. And she had been trying so hard to maintain an even temper. "I don't give a damn about the oil companies or you. The investigation is over and, quite frankly, for once your people were doing their jobs correctly. Now I know this may come as a shock to you, Allen, but the state of Alaska has a great many concerns to worry about other than the oil companies and the problems you seem to keep stumbling into. You spill your oil, and we clean it up. You violate lease agreements by building work sites in the restricted zones, and you'll probably be fined for that. You offend the native people, lose credibility, and the government has to smooth over all the rough edges. Well, I for one am over it."

Kay turned and didn't look back. A few feet away she saw Russ and Lela waiting for her, pretending to repack the

141

snowmobiles. They had heard the entire conversation, and Kay caught a brief glimpse of them smiling from ear to ear. Both continued to work and wouldn't look at her. "I'm sorry. I totally lost my temper, but I couldn't take any more from that guy."

Lela turned around and grabbed Kay's pack. Moving her hands efficiently, she strapped it to Kay's snowmobile. "I think short-tempered is good sometimes. I will remember that. My attempts to be nonconfrontational do not always work."

"I'm proud of ya, boss," Russ said, slapping Kay on the back. "Look, he's still standin' there with his mouth open."

Kay glanced over her shoulder. Allen hadn't moved an inch. He stood there squinting at them, mouth wide open. "He's finally found out how unimportant he is. At least to this team and what we have to do today."

They started out toward the Topagoruk River. The river ran north from Admiralty Bay south to Singiluk. After studying all the evidence and data provided by Grace and the Interior office, they believed strongly that the river was a perfect target for terrorists. It stretched for miles through the heart of the National Petroleum Reserve and served as a major source of water and food for many small Eskimo villages. The river was also a lifeline to a host of wildlife, including the endangered grizzly bear.

For most of the trip, the landscape was featureless — a vast ice field of frozen tributaries that ran inland from the Arctic Ocean. Occasionally, groves of pine trees pierced the rolling white hills and flat ice plains. If the chemicals were hidden underground, the team would never find the dumps. But given the weather conditions throughout the year, underground storage was highly unlikely. That's why they concentrated on the pine forests where drums of benzene could easily be hidden.

They made several stops through a few smaller pine groves in the first three hours of the trip. As they drew nearer to the river, the forested areas thickened. Russ waved for Lela and Kay to pull over.

"Let's check our maps here. We're getting close to the river, and I wanna give this entire area a thorough check. Do you agree, Kay?"

"Absolutely."

They pitched a tent in a matter of minutes and crawled inside. Lela heated some water, and Kay dug for some freeze-dried soup.

Spreading a large map across the nylon floor of the tent, Russ marked the forested grids along the seventieth parallel ten miles to the east and west of the river. "I'm thinking these grids are our best shot at finding something," he said. "Each grid is five square miles. There are six hot grids, if you will."

Kay nodded, running her finger across the map. "We can each cover two. One today and one tomorrow. We should find a place to camp overnight."

Lela handed Russ some coffee. "We can find a spot in the trees where there is some protection. If we connect all three tents together, we can concentrate what heat we can generate from the portable units we have."

"What do you think, Russ?"

"Lela's right. We should be fairly comfortable, and the weather's gonna hold. There's no precipitation predicted until late Friday. That's four days from now. I say we get a bite to eat right now and then find a place to call home for the next couple of days."

"What kind of soup is that, Kay?" Lela studied the packet. "Tomato?"

Russ gripped his coffee mug and warmed his hands. "Whatsa matter, Lela? Not one of your favorites?"

"Not in the least. What else do you have?"

Kay scrounged through the nylon pack. "Chicken noodle. That's pretty safe."

"Yes, give me that. Chicken noodle."

Kay glanced at Russ. "And you, my good man?"

"Have you got a ham sandwich?"

"Sorry, the deli's closed."

"Damn. Okay, just toss me that bag of pretzel nuggets I shoved in there. I'll munch on those for now."

"If I have to be on this trip, looking for this horrible poison, I'm glad it's with you two," Kay said while mixing her soup.

"I'll second that, Kay. You ladies are the best in the business."

Lela smiled. "And Grace told me over the phone that Mr. Bend was sometimes a neanderthal. But I think he is quite charming."

Russ's eyes bulged from his skull. "Neanderthal? She said that?"

Lela threw her head back and laughed. "No. It is only a joke, Russ. You really are very charming."

Russ shrugged. "My wife thinks so. But maybe she's been lyin', too."

They all laughed. After lunch, there was silence as they gathered their gear. Because they would be splitting up, everything they packed was critical. Russ spent a few minutes explaining some of the equipment they would be carrying.

"This is a handheld metal detector, compact — about the size of your standard hair dryer." Russ flipped a switch and the detector emitted an audible hum. "Whenever you're around any kind of metal, you'll hear this low hum. For example, it's detecting the metal in our boots and snowshoes. See the level here? It's picking up the metal, but the actual level is fairly low." Russ walked over to the snowmobiles. The small device emitted a piercing, high-pitched signal. "Look at the level now. The indicator is in the red zone. That's what we're looking for. A bunch of metal barrels that will push this indicator into the red zone."

"This will make our work much more efficient," Lela said while scrutinizing the detector. "You are a marvel, Russ."

"Thanks. Here's something else you'll both be taking with you." Russ handed them each a revolver. "I know Kay can handle one of these. What about you, Lela?"

"I am more accustomed to a rifle. But this will do."

"The guns will affect your metal detectors. But you'll still know if you come across a dump of benzene. The metal barrels will make this thing sing loud and clear. Trust me."

Kay slipped the gun back into its leather case. "Do you really think we'll need these, Russ?"

"If you come across a grizzly, a gun might be a handy item to have. Won't do much to stop an animal that size unless you empty the clip. But the gun will buy you some time if you need it. We also don't know *who* is out there. Maybe some of these crazy environmental terrorists. I don't know. But you can fire the gun as a signal for help, too. Anybody hears a gun, radio for assistance and move toward the signal. Don't forget about your flare guns."

"That's right. The flare guns can be seen for miles," Kay agreed. "Several other government search teams have been deployed on the west bank of the river. If you need help, everyone is on channel nine."

The three of them made some last-minute adjustments to their equipment, snowshoes, backpacks.

"Be careful, both of you," Kay said. "Don't take any chances. I'll see you back here at three o'clock sharp. That's exactly four hours from now."

Lela answered, "See you then."

Russ waved and smiled as Kay turned north. The hunt was on.

~ ~ ~ ~ ~

Kay's assigned territory was at the top of a rise north along the river's eastern shore. She unfolded her map and confirmed the direction with her compass. Her grid started about a quarter of a mile directly ahead where a large wooded area paralleled the shoreline.

The sun was finally shining after weeks of January darkness. Even though the weather was still bitterly cold, just seeing the sun was a relief. Strong winds whistled across the open space, and Kay was relieved when she finally reached the shelter of the woods. Abandoning her snowmobile, she set off on foot.

A constant low hum from the metal detector signaled that everything was normal. Kay continued deeper into the forest, keeping the edge of the tree line to the east in sight. She knew that any large chemical dump would need the cover of trees to conceal it, even if it was buried underground.

Struggling through the drifted snow, Kay felt a sudden rush of fear. Russ could take care of himself, but she worried about Lela. The last time she had sent a coworker into the Alaskan wilderness, it was with devastating results. It was like yesterday, that day of horror three years ago. Kay closed her eyes, and the old work camp buildings were right there — the original storage sheds and warehouses erected in the early seventies when the pipeline was built. Russ was talking to her, his voice as clear as if he was standing there at that moment.

"You did good, Kay. Real good." Russ took a quick look around. "Where's Lori?"

"Don't know. We split up about an hour ago, and I haven't seen her since."

"C'mon. We'll find her."

They ran toward the main building. The door had been left ajar. Inside, the room was strewn with remnants of the Alyeska crew's brief stay. Empty food containers, cigarette butts, tobacco juice stains, used-up fuel tins, pieces of wire, solder, and a few tools. They found everything but Lori.

They went back outside and followed the line of weather-battered equipment sheds until they ended near the edge of the woods at the camp's northernmost point. At the last shed they turned right. Up against the dirty gray building, barely visible in the shadows, they found Lori lying on her side. Kay saw a pool of blood seeping into the snow.

"Lori!" Kay knelt down and carefully turned her face up. She heard a faint moan.

"She's alive," Russ said, unclipping the walkie-talkie from his belt. "I'll get a copter in here right away."

As Russ's voice boomed into the radio, Kay held Lori's head.

She opened her eyes and smiled. "Kay — I must've fallen asleep on the job. Or did I?"

"Don't think so."

Lori coughed, her eyes blinking away the discomfort. "No. I bumped into one of them while they were leaving. They didn't take kindly to that. I tried to run . . ."

"Where are you hurt?"

"In the back, I think. Can't seem to feel my legs."

"Listen, you better be quiet. Russ's calling for help. We'll have you out of here in no time."

"Sure could use a cigarette."

"Not a good idea."

Russ returned with some blankets. "Help's on the way, kid."

Lori cradled herself against Kay and closed her eyes. "I'm tired."

The wind snapped a branch overhead, and Kay opened her eyes. The memory was gone. Nothing bad was going to happen to any of them, she thought. Everything was going to be okay.

Kay reached the top of the hill and scanned the area inside the tree line with high-powered binoculars. An hour later she sat down underneath a tall pine tree and ate some beef jerky. The stuff still turned her stomach, but over the years she had forced herself to tolerate the taste. There wasn't much you could take into the wilderness in the way of food that was nourishing and wouldn't spoil. Beef jerky had become one of the unfortunate compromises of her job. Along with trail mix, it was a wilderness staple.

When the shot was fired, Kay stopped mid chew. The sound echoed along the river, but she was sure it had come from the south. Not Lela, she prayed. Not Russ. Another gunshot. Yes, from the south and a little east. She scrambled to her feet and ran as fast as she could in her snowshoes, stumbling and falling until she reached her snowmobile a half-hour later. Her chest heaved as she struggled to catch her breath.

With the roar of the snowmobile in her ears, it was hard to hear anything else. Then Kay saw the flare burst through the trees, an orange trail of flames heading toward the sky. She opened the throttle and headed toward the smoke. Her heart raced and her mind flooded with a million thoughts. How maybe after all these years of failed relationships and disastrous trysts and love affairs she had finally found that once-in-a-lifetime love. Russ was okay, she convinced herself. He was always okay. But Lela was vulnerable because she made Kay vulnerable. Not Lela, she prayed.

The snowmobile bounced and skidded dangerously through the maze of trees until Kay saw the outline of people in the distance. Five people, maybe six, standing over something or someone. Oh my God. Not this. Not now.

That someone was Lela. Kay recognized her coat. She was slumped against a tree, and Russ was hovering over her. Kay abandoned the snowmobile and ran. She fell, struggled to her feet, and fell again. Kicking off her snowshoes, she attempted to crawl the last few yards, trying to yell out. But she was winded and no one saw her. They were all standing there looking down at Lela. Then she heard Lela laugh — that same musical, lighthearted laugh she had heard for the first time over a month ago. Lela was laughing. Lela was okay.

"Lela?" she managed to gasp. "Somebody tell me what happened."

As soon as Russ saw Kay, he broke into a run. "Are you hurt? Are you okay?"

"Fine. Just out of breath. What's going on? I heard the shots. Saw the flare."

"Calm down. Take a deep breath. Everyone's okay. Lela tripped over a benzene barrel and cut her leg. It's just a superficial scratch. Can you believe it? Her damned metal detector didn't even go off. She *tripped* over the freakin' dump."

"Tripped?" Kay saw Lela smile. Then Kay started to laugh, and everyone else joined in. Lela had tripped over the benzene dump.

"So much for these metal detectors," Russ said with disgust. "Maybe I can auction 'em off on eBay."

"For once Russell's equipment has failed," Lela said, shaking her head. "It was the spirit of the land that told me something was wrong. As I walked nearer to this place, I could feel it."

Kay collapsed on the ground at Lela's feet. "Everyone take a break. I want to talk to Lela." She waved her arms, shooing Russ and the other EPA team members away. "Please. Just for a few minutes."

"No problem, boss. We gotta radio this in anyway," Russ said, backing away. "I'll go get the camera equipment. Fellows, how about helpin' me?"

Lela pointed to the rip in her pants. "Now I have hurt myself. We are even."

"Is it bad?"

"No. It is just a scratch. Russ has already bandaged it."

"Lela, I love you."

149

"I love you, too, Kay."

"When I thought something had happened to you, I panicked. I couldn't imagine my life without you. I've never felt this way before. I've always been cautious with love . . . slow and overanalyzing every little thing. Trying to look for every wrong thing instead of every right thing. Now I realize it's because I never met the right person. Until now."

"Kay, you must be in love. You are babbling. It is not like you."

Kay slumped against the tree and rested her head on Lela's shoulder. "I don't know how we'll work things out between Barrow and Fairbanks. Somehow, we'll manage."

"Yes, we will."

"What about you, Lela? What about your people and what they will think if they find out about us?"

"They think I am crazy now. What will the difference be?"

"The difference will be that you'll be loving another woman."

"There have been other women. And it has probably already been talked about. But it has been a lonely road for me, and I cannot waste time worrying about what others might think. I stopped letting those things influence my decisions years ago. Besides, love should not be full of worry. It should be full of happiness. You should stop worrying, Kay. It is —"

Kay held up her hands, stopping Lela mid-sentence. "Don't even say it. That worrying's not like me. I worry all the time."

"I was going to say it. But it would have been a joke. I know you worry. That much I have figured out."

"What else have you figured out?"

"That you are my kindred spirit. That we will grow old together."

"I used to worry a lot about growing old."

Lela smiled. "Used to worry? Really?"

"Very funny. Yes, really. But not any more. With you I think I can grow old gracefully."

"Then we will be full of grace together."

Three days later, after scouring fifteen square miles of wilderness area, Kay, Russ and Lela headed back to Barrow. Other government teams that had been deployed along the river had found two more benzene dumps. All of the dumps had been reported to Washington, and the process of tracing the origins of the chemical dumps continued.

Arriving back in Barrow was like another homecoming for Kay. As she punched in the numbers for Grace's office in Washington, Lela poured two glasses of wine and stacked logs in the fireplace. It might as well be home, Kay thought. Everything about the small house was about Lela. From the Native American artifacts displayed on shelves to the hand-made woolen comforters of every color spread over the furniture, the house was Lela. Her heritage, gentleness, and spirit.

"Grace, Kay here. Just wanted to let you know we're back in Barrow. All of the reports have been sent to you by air — on the benzene and the Teshekpuk Lake investigation."

"I already have them, Kay. My staff is compiling the results and the official documents. Going to be a few days. Maybe longer. I'm thinking of making the benzene discoveries public."

"Won't that compromise the ongoing investigation?"

"Don't think so. We've got so much evidence now that tracing the origin of the benzene should be fairly simple. Actually, we've already narrowed it down to a foreign supplier. Had the benzene actually been dumped that would be another matter entirely."

"What kind of public release are you planning on this story?"

"That's where you come in. Schedule the next meetings with the Inupiat Northern Council and environmentalist groups in two weeks. I want it known that not only did the oil companies come up clean as a result of a government investigation, but that environmental sabotage was also avoided during that same investigation. The message is that this government cares about its land resources. We won't tolerate abuse of any kind, whether it's from the oil companies or terrorists."

"That's quite a PR message."

"I trust it will be a meaningful one to the people of northern Alaska."

"I'm sure it will. I'll set the meeting date and wait for the final reports."

"Good. By the way, I'll be in attendance at the meeting with the council."

"Great. I think that's very appropriate. I look forward to seeing you then."

"Will you go back to Fairbanks in the meantime?"

"Uh, no. Actually, I'm going to take a little time off. Might as well stay here in Barrow rather than having to travel back here in a couple of weeks anyway. I'll send Russ back to Fairbanks to take care of things at the office."

"Fine. I'll be in touch."

Kay hung up the phone and shook her head. "Grace never fails to surprise me."

"Is Grace going to be paying us a visit?" Lela asked, handing Kay a glass of wine.

"Yes. She wants me to set up a meeting in two weeks with the Northern Council. She's going to turn recent events into a public relations coup."

"It is not a bad thing, is it? There is good news for everyone."

"Yes, and Grace wouldn't miss out on a second of it. She

threw us both to the wolves for the first two meetings. But when it comes time for the victory dance, it's Grace's show all the way."

"It is a perk of being the boss."

"You're right. We are mere pawns in the grand scheme of things."

"Will Russ leave tomorrow?"

"Yes."

"I will miss him."

"He'll be happy. He hates the politics. He'll consider going back to Fairbanks a blessing. Personally, I'd be envious if it weren't for you."

Lela held up her glass. "Here is to us, Kay. It is good to be home."

"To us." Kay sipped some wine, then kissed Lela. "It's much better to taste the wine from your lips."

"Please have some more."

Kay kissed Lela again, pulling her closer. Lela's body felt like the fire, warm and inviting. She caressed Lela's hair, the coal-black strands flowing softly through her fingers. She felt Lela's breath on her neck, hungry kisses on her shoulders. Kay pulled Lela onto the rug in front of the fire, the snapping and crackling of the wood the music they would make love to.

"I want you, Kay."

"I want you, too. Today, tomorrow, the next day. We're on vacation for two weeks."

"It is like a dream."

"You are my dream. You've been my dream for a long time."

"First, I have a gift for you. To honor our first Valentine's Day together."

Kay flinched. "Oh my God. It is Valentine's Day, isn't it?"

"Yes, but I had time to do some present-making while you and Russ were in Washington. And here is my gift."

Lela handed Kay a package wrapped in red foil paper with a pink bow. Opening the box, Kay pushed aside the tissue paper to find a pair of mukluks. "My God, Lela. They're really beautiful."

"I made them for you, Kay."

"You made these? Thank you so much." Kay snatched the mukluks from the box. Each side displayed the beaded design of a bear's paw print. She held them up to her face. They were as soft as velvet. "I've always wanted a pair of these. But I could never find a pair I liked."

"These have moosehide bottoms and deerhide tops. Inside, they are lined with wool. You will find them excellent for snowshoeing."

"Lela, they're really special. I'm so sorry. I have nothing for you."

"Oh yes you do." Lela kissed Kay, her hands tousling Kay's hair. "You have something I desire more than anything else. Your love."

Kay pulled Lela into her arms and gave her a gift she would long remember.

The dream of that two-week vacation with Lela ended two days later with a phone call. When Kay heard her sister's voice on the other end of the line, she panicked. Julia would never call unless it was an absolute emergency. Something's wrong with Pop, she thought. There can't be any other reason.

"Julia, what's wrong?"

"Daddy is real sick, Kay. He's in the hospital."

"What happened?"

"He fell and hit his head. They say he's got a concussion or something like that. He hasn't spoken since he fell. He just lies there sleeping."

"When did he fall?"

"Three days ago."

"Three days ago! You've got to be kidding me. Why didn't you call me right away?"

"I was busy, Kay. At the hospital. Talking to the doctors. And I didn't know where you were."

"My office knows where I am."

"Yeah. They told me you were in Barrow. What are you doing there, anyway?"

"Working. That's what I'm doing, Julia."

"There's no need to yell at me. I did the best I could trying to find you. You don't know what's it's been like here. Jack is away, too. I'm here all by myself, and I'm scared. I'm doing the best I can for Daddy."

"I don't care. There's no excuse for waiting three days to call me."

"Sometimes you're such a brat, Kay. You can be so hateful. I can't call every town in the Alaskan wilderness trying to find you."

Kay listened to the sobs and suddenly felt guilty. "Look, I'm sorry. You're right. You did the best you could. I'll be home tomorrow morning. It'll be okay."

Chapter Nine

Kay could hardly believe it. Just four days earlier she was celebrating Valentine's Day with Lela. Today she was in a hospital waiting room in Fairbanks that was crowded with people lined up at the information desk. They were all jabbering at the same time, talking over one another. Kay fought a blossoming headache but patiently waited her turn. Twenty minutes later she was on the elevator to her father's room.

It was a private room with mint-green curtains. Her father appeared frail, his small frame dwarfed by the hospital bed and monitoring equipment. Kay sat down in the chair next to her dad. Holding her father's hand, she noted the bandages on the right side of his head.

"Pop, can you hear me? It's Kay."

His face showed no reaction. There was no change in his expression, not the slightest twitch of an eyebrow, no body movement at all. With long, slow breaths, his chest rose and fell at regular intervals. The machines beeped, and her mind buzzed with frightening thoughts. Then a cart rolled in front of the doorway and someone leaned partway into the room. "Newspaper?"

"No thanks," Kay answered. "Not today."

"I'll take one," another voice said.

Kay couldn't believe her eyes. It was Jack, her sister's husband. Clearly, it was going to be one of those days. There was no one else on earth Kay would rather not see — ever again.

The voice was deep, a low growl that made him sound like a Mafia boss. Her own private nickname for him was Marlon. "Kay, how's it going?" Jack was dressed in a gray suit with a white-and-navy striped tie. His shoes were oxfords, immaculately polished. A Rolex watch, one of his prized possessions, flashed when he moved his hand. His face was cleanly shaved, and every hair on his head was combed into waves of perfection.

"Just fine. You?"

"Perfectly well." Marlon played with his cuffs, twirling the gold cuff links between his fingers just like her sister twirled her hair. "Any word on your dad?"

"Not yet."

Shifting his weight to his other foot, Jack opened his suit coat, revealing a crisply starched shirt. "No change since yesterday?"

"I just got here this morning. He hasn't moved much or spoken. From what Julia told me, he's been like this for days."

"Have the doctors been in today?"

"No, not that I'm aware of. But then I'm not aware of very much."

Jack got bored with the cuff links and began fidgeting with

his silk tie. "Julie said they did an MRI and a CAT scan. He has a pretty bad concussion. The only other thing I can tell you is that they've given him some drugs to control the swelling in his brain."

"Thanks for the update. I plan to stay as long as I have to, until I get a chance to talk with the doctors."

"I understand. If you find out anything new, please let us know."

"Yeah, and I won't wait three days to call."

"Listen, Kay. Julie was a bit frantic about all of this. You know how she gets. It doesn't take much to unnerve her. As soon as your father was settled here and she was confident he was getting the best of care, she called your office and found out you were in Barrow. She rang you a couple of times at a hotel, but they said you'd checked out. Finally, she called Russ Bend and he gave her another number in Barrow. Some other colleague."

Kay felt guilty again. It actually may have taken Julia quite a few calls to finally reach her. "That's true. I'm sorry. I may have been difficult to track down. It's hard when you get a phone call out of the blue like that. Quite frankly, it scared the shit out of me."

"That's understandable, especially when you're on the road. What do they have you working on up in Barrow?"

"Some investigative projects. I can't talk about it much."

"Okay, that's cool. Well, Julie did honestly try to reach you. Whatever your problems are with one another — and let's not pretend they started when I married your sister — Julie would not purposely keep you in the dark about your father.

"I'm sure she wouldn't."

"Listen, you hang in there. I'm sure Pete's going to be fine. He's a pretty tough guy." Jack checked his three-thousand-dollar watch. "Gotta run. Catch you another time, okay?"

"Yeah, sure."

"Julie should be by this afternoon."

"I'll be here."

For a few hours, Kay sat by her father's bedside. She fell asleep twice and dreamed she was stranded in a snowstorm with Jack and Julia. Trapped inside a cave avalanched by snow, Julia calmly filed her nails and hummed the theme from *Gilligan's Island*. Meanwhile, Jack studied his Rolex-compass-three-time-zone watch, marking the passage of the hours. Kay was busy digging a tunnel with her gloved hands, trying to save them.

"Say, could I have a little help here?" she asked, gasping for each breath.

"Kay, I'd really like to help, but I don't want to ruin my nails," Julia pouted. "I just had them done last week."

"Hey, I'd help you too, Kay. No problem. But I don't want to damage my watch. We may need this compass."

Continuing to dig, Kay worked until the tunnel was as deep and dark as a tomb. Inside the tunnel she could hear the muffled sounds of Julia's and Jack's voices, yelling for her to dig faster. According to Jack's Rolex, time was running out.

Kay woke up suddenly. Her father was still sleeping peacefully. She wished him more pleasant dreams that she had just experienced. Rubbing her eyes, Kay got up and stretched. She checked her own watch. It was lunchtime. Since the doctors weren't due in until later that afternoon, Kay decided to take a break and grab something to eat. There was a popular deli about three bocks from the hospital, and she definitely needed the fresh air.

The day was overcast, and a few light flakes were falling. Kay walked toward the deli on the corner. She darted inside and headed straight for the counter to order. Suddenly, she was fighting hunger pangs and a growling stomach. Minutes later, she carried her tray toward the back of the restaurant.

She was just about to sit down when she was startled to hear someone calling her name. Turning one-eighty toward the sound of the voice, she immediately recognized Stef sitting two tables away with her new girlfriend. Kay invoked a fervent prayer to dematerialize to any other place on earth. A bad day had just gotten worse. Kay hadn't believed it possible.

Stef waved her over to their table. "Kay! Kay! C'mon over. Join us!"

There wasn't much Kay could do but inwardly surrender — to the bad day, the humiliation, to the crappy luck that had dogged her since her plane had landed in Fairbanks. She forced a smile and said pleasantly, "Stef, what a surprise. Nice to see you. And you, too, Jan."

Stef was beaming from ear to ear. "What are you doing here? I thought you were away."

"I just flew in from Barrow. My dad's sick."

"Oh my God. What happened?"

Kay glanced at Jan. She was sitting stiffly with her arms folded across her chest. She nodded at Kay with a strange expression, and Kay nodded back. "He fell and hit his head." Warily, Kay sat down. Jan's penetrating, dark eyes were still staring at her, making her uncomfortable.

"Is your dad going to be okay?" Stef asked.

Taking a sip of her jumbo Diet Pepsi, Kay glanced longingly at the turkey-bacon club sandwich on her tray. It looked delicious. But she wasn't going to enjoy it. Not one bit. "Well, he hasn't been conscious for days."

Stef put her hand on Kay's arm. "I'm so sorry. I love your dad. He's such a great guy."

Jan leaned against the wall, face twisted into a scowl. "Too bad about your dad," she said coldly.

Kay looked over at Jan and forced a smile. "Uh, thanks. I just got into town, so I haven't talked to the doctors yet. They're supposed to stop by this afternoon and give me a rundown on his condition."

"Call me," Stef pleaded. "As soon as you find out anything. Please."

"I will."

"Plus I'll stop by and see him tomorrow."

Jan tapped her fingers on the Formica tabletop. "We gotta be at Sara and Anne's tomorrow. Help them move."

"Oh, that's right. Well, they won't miss me for a half-hour or so. Kay's dad is like family to me. He lived with us for a couple of years."

"So you said," Jan agreed. "But we gotta do the move thing. They just helped us move."

Kay managed to take a bite of her sandwich. Her eyes shifted back and forth between Stef and Jan. The tension was palpable. Swallowing hard, Kay said, "You can stop by Thursday, Stef. He's going to be in for a while."

"Oh sure. Okay. After work."

"Work? Where you working now?" Kay asked.

Stef smiled and sat up straight. "The Gold Mine. I've been making pretty good tips."

The restaurant was a popular tourist spot. "You going back to school in the fall?"

"Maybe. If I can save up enough money."

Stef had been pursuing a special education degree with financial help from her father. Until Stef got bored and dropped out for a year. "No more help from your dad yet?"

"No. But I'm still working on him. I figure if I can pay for some of the next semester myself, he'll soften up a little. I've saved a couple thousand dollars."

Kay was surprised and proud. "Good for you."

Jan checked her watch. "Say, Stef. We really gotta get going."

"Oh yeah." Stef picked up her tray and lingered for a few seconds longer. "Well, it was nice seeing you Kay. I'll stop by to see your dad on Thursday."

"Thanks. Have a nice day. Good luck with move number two."

161

Wednesday, in between hospital visits, Kay decided to stop by the office. Forty-five minutes after walking in the front door, she had only managed to move about fifteen feet. Everyone in the office stopped to say hello and ask about her dad. When she did finally open her office door, Russ was sitting at her desk, filling out paperwork. She put her hands on her hips and smiled. Nose buried in forms, Russ was biting the tip of his number-two pencil. "Government paperwork is the worst, isn't it?"

"Hey, boss!" Russ got up and stepped away from the desk. "Was just trying to get some crap work done for you. All these requisition forms."

"Thanks. You're a pal."

"I would say welcome back, but I know your reasons for being back suck. How's your dad?"

"He's still unconscious. He had a pretty bad fall."

"I'm sorry."

"I'm headed back to the hospital in a few minutes. Just wanted to check in and see how things were going."

"They're goin' fine. But I have to say I don't know how you sit at this desk all day. The paperwork's enough to kill ya."

"You get used to it."

"How's Lela?"

"She handling the fort while we're away. The meetings with the Northern Council will be held in a couple of weeks. Grace is going to be there."

"Really?"

"She's going to personally handle the public relations spin."

"Oh, don't tell me. Forget the oil companies bein' the bad guys. How 'bout environmental terrorists? That's the real enemy."

"Exactly."

"Hail to the Interior Chief. She always finds a way."

"She does."

"You want me to stay here while Grace runs the show in Barrow?"

"Yes. No reason for you to be part of the big top show. It'll be circus enough. Besides, I can see you're getting pretty good at this paperwork."

"I'm goin' to sharpen another pencil right now. You take care. Call me and let me know about your dad before you head back to Barrow."

"I'll be in the office tomorrow and maybe even a few hours on Friday. I'd like to catch up on some things."

"Okay, great. I'll see you then."

Julia was filing her nails, and it was getting on Kay's nerves. It was Friday and Kay had left work at three o'clock to start the weekend early and spend some time with her dad. Her father had finally regained consciousness but was now napping. Kay sat on one side of the bed, flipping through *People* magazine. Julia was on the opposite side, intent on her beauty regimen. Before she started to file her nails, she had been plucking her eyebrows.

The reason for her father's fall had been uncovered. The medication he needed to control his Parkinson's disease had dangerously lowered his blood pressure. This caused him to black out and hit his head. To elevate his blood pressure, the doctors were trying a new medication and planned to monitor his progress for at least a few more days.

"Daddy seems much better, don't you think, Kay?"

"Yes, he does seem better. Just really tired."

"Jack and I think he should come home with us for a while before he goes back to that place you put him in."

Kay's face flushed with frustration. "That *place* provides excellent care."

"He fell there, didn't he?"

"Julia, he would have fallen anywhere. His damned blood pressure was practically zero over zero."

"You don't have to swear at me."

"Oh for crying out loud." Kay closed the magazine and rolled it into a tube. She got up and peered out the window, tapping the magazine against the palm of her hand. The sun was out and the temperature was a balmy thirty degrees. "Pop will be fine when he gets out of here. No reason to uproot him again. Besides, we should ask him what he wants."

"He always does what you say."

"Unless we go to court."

Julia stopped filing her nails and glared at Kay as though she had just been viciously slandered. "Going to court was necessary. Daddy needed help."

"No it wasn't. It was all about you and me, Julia. It had nothing to do with what was best for Pop." Kay stood stiffly with her arms folded, the magazine tucked under her chin. Julia had started to twirl her hair again, the same way she'd done when she was a kid. "You could never accept that Pop and I had something special growing up. That we connected."

"Connected? You were the son he never had. This unbelievable tomboy who would go fishing and hunting with him. I did normal girl things."

"And now we get right to the heart of the matter. What's normal and what's not."

"I didn't make the rules for normal society, Kay."

"Rules? You just don't get it, do you? I'm your sister, Julia. That's the only thing that's supposed to matter."

"It did matter to me." Julia answered sullenly, crossing her legs. "But you never had to put up with all the stuff I had to listen to from my friends. How you were a dyke and all."

"Did that cramp your style? Did it stop you from getting dates or going to the prom, Julia?"

"And that's another thing. All my friends — and even

164

Mom and Daddy — called me Julie. With you, it's always been Jule-ya."

"I love the name Julia. When you were born and Mom and Pop brought you home, the first thing they did was tell me your name. Julia. It sounded so beautiful." Kay turned back toward the window. "And what a beautiful baby you were. Mom and Pop were so proud. I ran and told all my friends that I had a baby sister named Julia."

"You never told me that."

"I should have."

"We're just different, Kay. We might as well face it."

"Does that mean we have to be enemies? Can't we work out the differences? Other people seem to do it all the time."

"I don't think of us as enemies."

"Really?"

"No, I don't. Just because we don't get along doesn't mean we're enemies."

"That's good to know."

"And really, Kay, I don't care that much about the lesbian thing. I wish you weren't one, but I guess you can't really help it."

Kay shook her head. "No, I can't."

"Well, sometimes I think you wish I wasn't me. But I can't help it either, can I?"

"No, I guess you can't." Turning away from the window, Kay noticed that Julia had started buffing her nails. She had a moment of clarity as she watched her sister — and the answer seemed simple. Neither one of them could change who they were, and neither one of them could change what had happened between them. Kay pulled a chair up to the window and sat down. Leaning her elbow on the window sill, she let her mind drift back to the courtroom four years earlier where all the acid feelings between her, Julia, and her brother-in-law had erupted like a volcano.

~ ~ ~ ~ ~

165

The courtroom on her side was empty except for the first row where Alex and Pat sat. The maple benches on the other side of the courtroom, directly behind her sister and brother-in-law, were filled with distant family relations, friends, and coworkers of both her sister and brother-in-law — along with many people she'd never seen before. Sitting in the witness chair beside the judge, Kay felt very much alone. She smiled at her father to reassure him, and he bent his head in shame — and pain. Shame because he could no longer care for himself. Pain because of Kay's pain. He'd told Kay he hadn't wanted this courtroom scene, didn't want Kay to be hurt. He wanted Kay to handle his affairs but had been judged unable to decide for himself. So the court would decide at her father's expense. And, as Kay was about to find out, at her own.

Kay's questioning, at the hands of her sister's lawyer, had begun about a half-hour before. The thirty-something preppy lawyer, Raymond Collier, was one of her brother-in-law's best friends. His initial questions concerned Kay's relationship with her father, her sister, and her mother, plus questions about work and career plans.

There had been a brief recess, and then her sister's lawyer slid out from behind the front table and approached, his hands punched into an expensive Italian suit. Collier swaggered and cleared his throat.

"Do you own your own home, Miss Westmore?"

"Yes."

"Do you live alone?"

"No."

"With whom do you reside?"

"A friend. Barbara Reynolds."

The tall, solidly built man turned toward the judge. "A friend?"

"Correct."

"Isn't it true that Barbara Reynolds is your lover and that you, Miss Westmore, are a lesbian?"

Kay's lawyer, Constance Steward, jumped from her seat. "Objection, Your Honor. This line of questioning is irrelevant. Miss Westmore's lifestyle has no bearing on her ability to make decisions concerning her father's welfare."

The judge leaned forward, his dark eyes flashing annoyance. "The attorneys will please approach the bench."

As the judge and attorneys exchanged words, Kay glared at her sister. There seemed to be no remorse in her eyes, no regret on her face. Her brother-in-law was smirking, clearly pleased with the new line of questioning.

Constance Steward returned to her chair. She did not look happy.

"Objection overruled," the judge said. "You may answer the question, Miss Westmore."

Kay concentrated, with all her will, on remaining steady. "That's correct," she said calmly. "We've been together for four years."

"So you acknowledge your homosexuality, Miss Westmore?"

"Yes."

"Is Miss Reynolds here today?" Collier asked, pointing toward the open courtroom.

"No. She's working."

"And prior to your relationship with Miss Reynolds, how many other lesbian affairs have you had?"

"Objection, Your Honor."

"Overruled. You may answer."

Kay was infuriated. "I don't remember," she snapped.

"You don't remember, Miss Westmore? Would you describe yourself as promiscuous then?"

"Of course not."

"Have you ever had several lovers at once?"

"No."

"Have you ever gone to bars to pick up other women?"

"Have you?" Kay asked sarcastically.

Collier laughed, his blond mustache twitching with delight. "Well, now if I did, Miss Westmore, it would be considered normal, wouldn't it?"

Kay didn't respond. She glanced at her father. His head was buried in his hands. His shoulders were shaking with tears. Kay looked at her sister. "You're the one who's hurting Pop, Julia. Look at him."

"Objection. The witness wasn't asked to speak," Collier said.

"Miss Westmore, please confine your answers to Mr. Collier's questions," the judge instructed.

"Have you ever gone for any kind of counseling, Miss Westmore?"

Kay couldn't believe it. Her sister hadn't held anything back. "Yes."

"Was it voluntary?"

"Not exactly."

"Who sent you?"

"My mother."

"For what reason?"

"Because . . ." Kay stopped. She felt so betrayed.

"We're waiting, Miss Westmore."

"My mother didn't agree with my lifestyle."

There was a low murmur throughout the courtroom.

"What about your father?"

"My father's always accepted me for who I am."

"Did he object to the idea of counseling?"

"It wasn't his idea."

"That wasn't my question, Miss Westmore. I asked if your father objected to your mother's recommendation that you obtain the services of a professional counselor?"

Kay bowed her head. "No."

Collier turned on his heels. "That's all, Miss Westmore. I have nothing further."

Two days later, the judge made his decision. Kay's father was to live with Jack and Julia. They were to be his legal guardians — in control of all his finances and the home care he needed. That arrangement lasted less than a year. As soon as Jack had found a way to hide her father's money in his own investments and real estate deals, they put Kay's father in the county home.

Outside the window, a large truck clanked its way down a hospital alley to pick up the day's trash. Kay glanced toward the alley and watched the green sanitation truck back up to the Dumpster. Shaking off the bad memories, Kay looked over at her father, still asleep and unresponsive. He was the only person who had mattered back then, at least to her. And he was the only person who mattered now.

Kay sat in her apartment, staring at the muted television set. There was never anything worth watching on a Friday night. In some ways, it was good to be back in Fairbanks. But she missed Lela. She had just hung up the phone after filling Lela in on her father's improving condition. The sound of Lela's voice made her long for those misty-gray eyes and the feel of Lela's arms around her. The last seven weeks had been running through her mind like an eight-millimeter film, flashing blurred images of her time with Lela. Every moment seemed blurred because every moment had caught her by surprise. Lela in the airport the first day they met, Lela in the truck driving down ice-pitted roads, Lela in her arms on a cot during nights that seemed to last forever. She would head back to Barrow next week, and the thought of being with Lela outweighed all other emotions. The success of everything else she had worked for during the last two months mattered little. The meeting with the Inupiat Northern Council, the presence of Grace Perry in Barrow, the public relations coup that was being carefully orchestrated by the Department of the Interior — all of these events seemed insignificant. Memories of Lela's calm voice, warm smile, long raven hair, and soft caresses in the early morning dominated her thoughts and kept her sane.

But suddenly, almost unwillingly, her thoughts turned toward her sister and their conversation earlier that day. Julia's comments about the embarrassment of having a dyke for an older sister stung to the core. Kay tried hard to remember Julia's high-school days, when Kay was already in college. The private liberal arts college Kay attended and the small city high school were only blocks away. The high-school students often attended college fraternity and sorority parties, held off campus. This fact led Kay and Julia to one of their most painful confrontations.

Kay was standing outside the sorority house waiting for Carmen. They were going dancing at a gay bar a few miles outside of town. The Saturday night party at the sorority was in full swing. Looking up, Kay could see the students on the outside balcony, hanging over the railing, some talking and some singing to the blaring music. Carmen was a sorority sister, but not Kay. She couldn't stand the snootiness of these women — or the pretentiousness of being a sorority sister. All of it turned her stomach. Carmen was a breath of fresh air and clearly her own woman. She had come out only after being accepted into the sorority, and her coming out had been a source of discomfort to her sisters ever since. Carmen was on the inside, but only as an outsider. Kay admired Carmen for her ability to let it all roll from her shoulders. In fact, the sisters had become a constant source of amusement for Carmen, and she always filled Kay in on the daily sorority soap opera.

Carmen was a good friend but perpetually late. Kay sighed

and sat down on the front steps. A few minutes later she wanted to run away, far away, from that front porch stoop. She couldn't believe her eyes. Julia was strolling along the sidewalk to the sorority house. She was laughing and joking with a group of male and female friends, all making their way to the party.

Kay got up and looked at the front door, wondering if she could slip inside and quickly leave out the back. But it was too late. Kay turned toward the sidewalk, filled with indecision. Julia was standing in front of the house looking directly into her eyes.

"Uh, Julia. Hello. I'm waiting for a friend."

Julia's friends were noticeably uncomfortable. They stared at the sidewalk, hands inside pockets, whispered comments passing between them.

"We're here for the party," Julia said quietly. "I . . . I didn't know you'd be here."

"Really, I'm just waiting for Carmen. She should be out any second."

Julia started twirling her hair. "Oh yeah. I heard about her."

"Heard what?"

"Just heard about her."

"What? That she's a dyke like me?"

"Cut it out, Kay. My friends are here. I don't want to talk about this now."

Kay was filled with anger. Julia never introduced her to her friends, not even when they came to their own house. "I'm sorry I'm such an embarrassment to you, Julia. But you're the one who told your friends about me. Why the hell'd you do that if you're so freaking embarrassed?"

"I didn't have to tell them anything, Kay. Everyone knows about you. Like it's no big secret, okay?"

Julia's voice was filled with disdain and a hurtful loathing. The sound cut Kay to pieces. "You shouldn't be here. You're underage." That was all Kay could think of to say.

"Shut up, Kay. You're not my mom."

"Kay, baby. You ready to go and shake your booty?"

Kay felt Carmen's hand on her shoulder. "Yeah, I'm ready to go. There's no one to talk to here."

When she heard the thumping sound, Kay stared curiously at the television screen, until she remembered that the sound was muted. When the noise startled her again, she realized that the disturbance was coming from her front door. Who could it possibly be? She had no recollection of inviting anyone over.

Kay squinted through the peephole, and her jaw dropped. "What in the world?" she muttered.

Opening the door, Kay stared and said nothing. Stef was bundled up tight in a navy parka. A few hours ago, the wind had picked up and the temperature had dropped at the same time. She looked half frozen. "Hi ya, Kay. Can I talk to you for a minute?"

"Of course. C'mon in. You look miserable."

"I walked here."

"Walked? Have you lost your mind? It's two freaking miles."

"Yeah, well I need the exercise."

Kay glanced at Stef's size-ten frame. "Like heck you do. Something's wrong. What is it?"

"Can I sit down?"

"I'm sorry. Of course you can. Here, let me take your coat. Would you like something to drink? Coffee? Hot chocolate?"

"Some hot chocolate would be nice."

"Coming right up."

A few minutes later, Kay handed Stef a cup of steaming chocolate topped with marshmallows. "This ought to thaw you out."

172

"Thanks. Kay, what's wrong with your TV? There's no sound."

Kay shook her head and chuckled softly. "Honey, it's on mute."

"Oh. I thought it was broken. Why do you have it on mute?"

"Never mind." Kay punched Power, and the television screen went dark. Sipping some black decaf coffee, she sat on the sofa next to Stef. "What's up?"

"I wanted to apologize for lunch the other day."

"What do you mean, 'apologize'?"

" 'Cause Jan wasn't exactly friendly. In fact, she was in a real pissy mood. And, like there's never any warning when she gets like that. One minute she's charming as hell and the next minute she's crabby."

"Why do you think that is?"

"Well, I kinda have it figured out now. I've been thinking about it a lot. Reading articles on the Internet. It's jealousy. This obsessive thing she has."

"Obsessive?"

"With me, Kay. Knowing my every move. Getting hot and bothered over nothing."

Kay swallowed hard. She couldn't believe her ears. Stef's words were a frightening reminder of her own experiences with Barbara. "Give me some examples."

"Like last week when you sent me that birthday card. Jan was real snippy about it. Then my friend, Nancy, from school called to wish me a happy birthday, and Jan practically freaked. We were supposed to go out for dinner to celebrate but ended up having this huge fight. It was like this really big drag for two days after my birthday. Finally she got over it."

"How long has she been like this?"

"That's the part I don't get. She was never this way before we started to live together. But since we got the apartment, she's been acting like a real dope. I mean, I don't give her any

173

reasons to be jealous. But it's like she finds them anyway. And then she does this brooding thing that's really a downer. That's when she's not yelling about something."

"You can't ignore this. You've got to make her go to counseling as soon as possible."

Stef shrugged. Her eyes glistened and her lower lip trembled. "I don't know, Kay. Maybe it's not even worth it."

"Not worth it? You've got to at least try to work it out. Especially if you love her. It sounds like she could use some help, and maybe you're the person who can convince her to get some."

"That's not exactly what I meant. I think it's not worth it because I'm pretty sure I made a mistake."

"Mistake?"

"Yeah. My mistake was leaving you, Kay. I don't know what I was thinking."

Suddenly Kay felt indignant. All those months of slowly losing Stef came flooding back in an instant and hit her full force in the gut. "I'll tell you what you were thinking. That you were bored, that the routine of our life together had become stagnating for you. You wanted to be with women your own age, not with an older lover helping take care of her sick father. Does any of this sound familiar?"

"Listen, I know that's what I said. It's everything that I told you. But I was wrong. And I want to come home, Kay."

Kay got up, and her legs nearly buckled. She steadied herself, pacing the foyer behind the sofa. She was sure this was all a big joke or a dream and that at any moment someone was either going to tell her the punch line or she was going to wake up relieved that it had all happened in her head. She glared at Stef in disbelief. A part of her wanted to scream the anger she was feeling. A part of her wanted to cry more of the same tears she had already cried. An angry voice in her head kept saying, How dare you? Then her real voice said, "This is nonsense. You can't do this." Kay spun around until she faced

Stef again. "You can't do this to yourself or to me. You can't walk out of my life and then walk right back in again because you didn't think things through. It's not fair."

With the sleeve of her shirt, Stef wiped tears from her face. "Fair? Is it fair to keep this to myself? To not tell you what an asshole I've been? Regardless of what you think of me, Kay, I needed to tell you this. If you don't want me back, just say so. Like it'll be okay, okay? It's just no freaking big deal."

Kay knelt in front of Stef, squeezing both her hands. They were soft and warm from the mug of cocoa. "Yes, it is a big deal, so just be quiet with that kind of nonsense. The thing is, it's not a simple matter of wanting you back, Stef. Do you know how many tears I cried, how many prayers I said, how often I cursed you under my breath for leaving me? I wanted you back, Stef. But you left, and I had no choice but to move on. With my life and my feelings."

"Maybe you just need some time to think about things like I did." Tears rolled down Stef's cheeks and she buried her face in her hands. "I know we could be happy again."

"Maybe. Maybe we could." Sitting on the floor, Kay rested her head on Stef's knee. She needed to tell her about Lela, let her know that there was zero chance of them ever getting back together again. But she wasn't sure she could say those words, not just yet. She couldn't imagine telling Stef, You can never come back. "But are you sure, Stef? Can you honestly say that you were happy those last months we were together — before you met Jan, before you told me that you were leaving? If you had been truly happy, you never would have left."

"I got confused. You know how I am. My mouth says stuff before my brain can sort things out."

"Then it's both our faults. We should have talked things through instead of yelling at each other."

"I agree."

"Go home, Stef. Think about all of this. Talk to Jan about

175

the counseling. Maybe the happiness you think you've lost is where you live right now. You need to sort this out before you do anything else."

"I'll go home. Thanks for listening." Stef grabbed her coat. "And if I made a complete ass out of myself telling you this stuff, it was worth it. Because you're worth it."

"Listen, wait. I'll drive you home."

"No. I'll call Jan. Ask her to pick me up at the drugstore. It's only a couple of blocks from here. She and I need to talk anyway."

"Are you sure?"

"I'm sure. Good night, Kay."

Kay shut the door. She was still in shock. Slumping into the sofa, her thoughts drifted back to Barb. *Obsessive, jealous, suspicious* — those were words that reminded her of Barb. Could it be possible that Stef had met someone just like her? Barb's behavior had been chaotic and frightening, and Stef's description of Jan's behavior paralleled Barb's earlier behavior exactly.

Grabbing a throw pillow, Kay rested her head on the arm of the sofa. Memories of Barb came back in precise detail. Flashes of anger, yelling, and throwing things. The angry threats and intentional disruptions at parties or with friends that came without warning. The accusations and innuendo whenever Kay's movements couldn't be accounted for every second of the day.

It wasn't as though their relationship had ever been perfect. Somehow they managed to stay together for just over five years. During that time Barb had strayed several times, seeking out other lovers, especially during Kay's long absences into Alaska's many national and state parks. But after Barb strayed, she always came back, holding on to Kay tighter than before. More controlling. More determined to keep Kay to herself — away from parties, away from family events, away from life. They did everything together or nothing at all. And while Barb had her solitary forays out into the world, when Kay wasn't traveling, she stayed home. Cleaned. Cooked. Worked. Work had been her only escape. And jogging.

Kay had jogged along the Chena River. She often ran two or three miles. But that day she jogged five . . . six . . . seven. By the time she got home it was much later than usual. Barb was waiting for her at the top of the porch steps. Arms crossed in front of her. Anger leaping from her eyes.

"Where've you been?"

"Running."

"You're late."

Kay shrugged. "I went farther than I usually do."

"Liar."

"Barb, for Christ's sake! Will you look at me? I just jogged seven fucking miles. Now get out of my way."

Barb stood firm, blocking Kay's way inside the building. "Who is she?"

"Who's who?"

"The bitch you're fucking behind my back. That's god-damned who!"

"You're crazy. Get out of my way."

"Why are you doing this to me, Kay? I love you."

"I'm not doing anything, Barb. You won't let me do anything. And it's killing our relationship. Don't you see that?"

"I only see you're trying to dump me."

"No. I'm trying to run away from you, but I can't seem to

run far enough. Five miles. Ten miles. A thousand fucking miles! It doesn't matter. It'll never be far enough."

She pushed by Barb, running up the stairs into the apartment. Running away. The voice behind her always there. "I'll never let you go, Kay. Never."

Chapter Ten

The waiter brought their food and then stood there staring at them. Kay and Alex stared back.

"Can I get you ladies anything else right now?"

It was Saturday night and the Mexican restaurant was packed. Every two minutes the reservation host blared someone's name over an open microphone. Fixated on the waiter's diamond-studded nose ring, Kay was unable to answer the simple question.

"I think we're fine for now," Alex said. "We'll let you know if we need anything. Thanks."

Kay stared at the plate in front of her and tried to remember where their conversation had left off. Her head was a useless jumble of confusion. "What was I telling you?" She stared at Alex blankly.

Alex's deep blue eyes stared back with concern. "You were telling me about Stef's visit last night. I just can't believe she showed up at the apartment like that, Kay. And then to declare that she wants you back after all she put you through. Good God," Alex groaned, stabbing at her taco salad. "I could just throttle her."

"That makes two of us." Kay stared at the cheese-and-bean burrito. Her stomach did a slow turn. She pushed the plate away.

Alex squeezed Kay's hand. "You must be angry. I can tell you're angry."

"How can you tell?"

"You just pushed your plate away and you're not going to eat anything. You're going to sit there and watch me stuff my face."

"You do the cooking for me, Al, and I'll eat. Your cooking is the only thing that could make me feel like eating right now."

Alex smiled. "It's a deal. You come for dinner tomorrow night. Pat wants to see you anyway."

"How is Pat?"

Alex shrugged and stabbed another piece of lettuce. "Pat moves to the beat of a different drummer. You know that. Every day is an adventure."

"I'm having my share of adventure. Seems only fair that you have yours."

"Listen, between you and Pat, my life is hardly dull. This afternoon Pat was busy setting the garage on fire."

"What?"

"She fancies herself the 'man' around the house, you know. Leather tool belt and all."

"Was that something you bought her for Christmas?"

"Hell, no. She went to the local hardware store and maxed

out one of our charge cards. Then she insisted we have a shed built in the backyard."

"She wants to burn that down, too?"

"Wouldn't be surprised. This afternoon she was using a soldering gun next to a pile of old turpentine rags. *Poof!* Next thing you know the damn garage is parched. Just the one wall, mind you, but I've got a couple more gray hairs."

"So do I. This thing with Stef came way out of left field. This is one adventure I could have done without."

"Because you still care about her."

"Of course I still care about her. But I've gone on, Al. It was hell trying to put this loss behind me. Then I met Lela, and love was something I could hold on to again. I know that meeting Lela was immediate and sudden, and, believe me, it scares me to death. But when Stef told me she'd made a mistake I wanted to ask her, 'Why? Why?' Then I wanted to scream, 'Stupid, stupid, stupid. All that pain. The agony of letting go. And overnight you come back into my life expecting me to find my feelings again. Expecting me to back-peddle into the past just like that.' "

Kay snapped her fingers and slapped the table with her hand. "I am so angry. I'm angry with myself for all of the mistakes I made with Stef. I'm angry with her for not hanging in a little longer. Maybe we could have worked things out."

"Did you tell her about Lela?"

"No. I was in too much shock. Then I started worrying about Stef. The things she said about Jan. They reminded me so much of Barb."

"Stef's a big girl, and she's made some choices. They may have been bad ones, but it's not your responsibility. You deserve to be happy now."

"That doesn't mean I don't love Stef. That I don't care what happens to her."

"Of course not. But it's not like you're going to take her back or something like that. Are you?"

"No."

"Then all you can do is be her friend."

"And that means being honest with her, which I should have been when she came over last night. I should have told her about Lela right away. I don't know why I didn't."

"Like you said, you were caught off guard."

"Damn, I miss Lela. I wish she were here right now. I can hardly wait for you to meet her."

"I can hardly wait too. When are you heading back to Barrow?"

"Next week."

"Everything will be fine, Kay. Like I said, Stef's a big girl. She can take care of herself."

"I was a big girl too. But that didn't stop Barb from making my life miserable."

"That's true. But history doesn't always have to repeat itself. Maybe Jan's just nervous about the new relationship."

"I honestly don't know. But it's pretty much up to Stef now, isn't it? To make her own decisions. Just like I did with Barb."

"I agree. C'mon, let's forget dinner and go do some shopping. We've still got a couple of hours before the stores close. You said you wanted to get your dad something."

"He needs some new slacks."

"Then let's go spend some money. I don't know about you, but that always makes me feel better."

When Kay arrived at the hospital on Sunday, her father was sitting up in his bed eating chocolate pudding. The rest of the lunch on his tray was gone.

"Is that dessert, Pop?"

"Yes. I was hungry."

"Pop, the one thing you've always had is a healthy appetite. How are you feeling today?"

"Better. I can go home tomorrow."

"Hey, that's great news."

"Why didn't you tell me about Stef?"

Kay was stunned. It was just like her father to be so direct. "Actually, I hadn't gotten the chance. It just happened. She only moved out a few weeks ago."

"Julie told me Stef moved in November."

"Yeah, I guess it has been a few months. Seems like yesterday."

"I'm sorry."

"So am I."

Some pudding dribbled onto her father's chin. "I hated to hear about it from Julie. Of all people. But, you know, she seemed really upset for you."

Wiping her father's chin with a Kleenex, Kay felt guilty. "I should have told you first, Pop. It wasn't right that you had to hear it from Julia."

"I love both my daughters. But Julie is sometimes harder to love."

Sitting down in the vinyl chair next to her father's bed, Kay stared at him in wonderment. This was the most substantive conversation they'd had in years. "I love Julia too. I just wish she'd accept me for who I am. It would make things so much easier on us."

"I don't like to see you both fighting. And I get angry with her, too. But I'm too old and tired to fight any more battles."

"You don't have to fight those battles anymore, Pop. Julia and I need to make some kind of peace. It's up to us. We're big girls now."

Tears welled in her father's eyes. "Your mother could handle Julie better. The only thing I can do is tolerate her and try to love her as best I can."

"Mom would just give us that look. Remember?"

Her dad laughed, his eyes crinkling into small slits.

"I remember."

"Mom only ever had to use looks and words. Mothers are good for stuff like that."

Her father pushed his tray table away. "Are you going back to Barrow?"

"Next week. Have some business to finish up there, and then I'll be home. Should only be there another week or so before I get stuck behind a desk again."

"You should ask Washington for your old job back. You liked it better."

"I do miss the travel. But I'll be okay. I'm going to ask Washington for some increased staffing at the office. I probably won't get it, but it's worth a try. If I can get help with some administrative type stuff, I'll be able to travel again."

"I don't like it when you're gone. But it's what makes you happy." Leaning his head back on his pillow, her father looked tired. "Stef made you happy."

"She did. But life goes on." A few minutes later, her father was snoring softly. She also drifted on the edges of sleep, thinking about next week. Happily, she fantasized about the trip back to Barrow on Tuesday — and back into Lela's arms.

Chapter Eleven

Kay peered out the kitchen window. Lela was stacking wood, piling the last few logs on the top row. As she watched Lela work, Kay poured coffee into a stoneware mug and stirred in some cream. Being reunited with Lela had been everything she'd hoped. Last night they had stayed awake for hours — making love, laughing, talking. It had been easy to forget about Stef, her father, the piles of paper waiting for her back in Fairbanks. For one long beautiful night it had been so easy to forget.

A loud crash at the side of the house startled Kay. She set the coffee cup on the counter and peered out the window. Lela was watching what was left of the woodpile roll down a steep snowbank. The logs picked up speed and smashed into a line of pine trees at the edge of the woods. Throwing her hands up in frustration, Lela stood stiffly, mouth wide open. Kay chuckled and threw on her coat.

The sky was gray with snow clouds, and the air was damp. She could smell the snow coming. It was going to be a vicious storm.

"Better go fetch that wood, babe. We'll need it when the storm gets here."

Lela squinted at Kay, hands on hips. "Fetch? Am I a mush dog now?"

Gathering Lela in her arms, Kay kissed Lela's cheek. "You're as warm as a mush dog, but much prettier."

"Thank you. Now if I can only learn to stack wood."

Kay gazed at the scattered wood and shook her head. "You've made quite a mess out here, but I think we can manage to clean it up." Kay bent over to pick up a log and felt a foot at her backside. Suddenly, she was facedown in the snow. "Hey!"

"So, I have made a mess you say? Now look at you. You are a mess and we are even." Lela scooped up some snow with her hands. The white stuff was quickly airborne, landing on Kay's head.

"Now cut that out! I was only kidding about the woodpile." Kay scrambled to her feet, and another snowball narrowly missed her arm. "Really, I surrender. Honest!"

"You have no fight in you, Kay? You surrender! That is pitiful."

"Pitiful? Fine. That does it." Kay packed her own snowball and took aim. It hit Lela in the shoulder.

"Ha! That was a sissy throw."

"Sissy? I don't think so."

"Here you are, this strong, independent woman. And you throw snowballs like a two-year-old."

"I do not!"

Lela was laughing hard now and running toward Kay. Tackling her at the knees, Lela pulled Kay with her as they rolled halfway down the hill. They were both laughing now. Lela ended up on top of Kay, pinning her down with her arms. "You are soft inside, Kay. You only pretend to be strong."

"I can't fight back when you make me laugh like this. Besides, I like you on top."

Lela bent over and whispered in Kay's ear. "Ah, so that is it. You like me on top. Yes, I like it too. Especially when you are inside of me."

"We could be doing this in front of a nice, warm fire."

"Then do you give up? Do you surrender to the stronger spirit?"

"I surrendered to your spirit the day we met."

"Yes, you did. I could feel it then. I knew your heart was mine to have."

"How did you know that?"

"It was written in your eyes and I could hear it in your words. When you spoke, your heart spoke, too."

"Well, you're lucky that I came along. Lucky that I was so transparent, that my heart almost leapt from my throat when we first met. Without me, you could have ended up with Thaddeus."

Lela started to laugh so hard she lost her balance and fell over next to Kay. Kay wiped the tears from her eyes and got up, seizing the advantage. She slid on top of Lela and kissed the laughter from her lips. Their mouths were hungry for each other. Those long days away from Lela, Kay had dreamed of their kisses, their touches.

"How much did you miss me?" Kay asked, kissing Lela's neck.

"I missed you as much as I have missed Robert all these years. As much as a young Eskimo boy misses the hunt. It is said that when the spirit of the land speaks and there is no answer from those who leave their footpath, then the signs and what was spoken are lost to the heavens forever. And that is how I felt without you. Like all my words and all my movements were lost to the heavens."

"I want your words and movements to stay here on earth."

"It is time to go inside, Kay."

"You pour the wine. I'll bring the wood."

Kay only made it a few feet inside the front door. Lela was waiting with a glass of wine. The firewood hit the floor with a loud *thud*. Kay stepped forward into a kiss. Lela's lips and tongue tasted like Chardonnay.

"I cannot wait. I want to make love to you now." Suddenly, Lela's hands were at Kay's jeans. In a few moments they were unbuttoned and being eased past Kay's hips. Lela's tongue found its mark and Kay closed her eyes, her knees weak with excitement. Then Lela was inside of her, stroking her at the same time her tongue continued its magic between her thighs. Kay held on to Lela's shoulders for support. She heard herself moan, and then she came with a force that buckled her knees. Holding her up, Lela continued to stroke her until she came again. Lela grabbed her around her waist and held her there as the orgasm pounded through her. "Lela, darling, that was lovely."

"You are lovely."

"No, I'm numb from the knees down."

"Do you need help walking?"

Kay ran her fingers through Lela's coal-black hair. "No, because I'm going to come down there and fuck you in the middle of the floor."

"I am waiting."

By Wednesday the storm was over. That evening Lela and Kay managed to negotiate the snow-covered roads to have dinner with Grace downtown. The meeting with the Northern Council and the press was scheduled for the next day. Grace was in a foul mood. She had been stuck overnight at the tiny airport outside of Barrow and had been forced to sleep in a chair.

"I hate snow. I'm going to move to a warm climate and stay there," Grace complained. "My neck and back are killing me. Finally, at two o'clock this afternoon they managed to get me to my hotel."

"Sorry you had a bad night." Kay smiled at Grace and shrugged.

Grace gave Kay a funny look. Lela had begun talking about the Northern Council, and the waiter was serving water. Kay smiled again, sipped some water, and buried her nose in the menu. She had the odd feeling that Grace knew about Lela and her. It didn't seem possible, since Grace had only been with them for a total of fifteen minutes. But Kay never put anything past Grace. She had an uncanny intuition about people, politics, and intrigue. Kay could feel tiny droplets of perspiration forming above her brow. Her cheeks were hot and probably flushed, giving Grace even more ammunition for her suspicions.

"Aren't you feeling well, Kay?" Grace asked, tossing her menu aside.

"Uh, well, I may be coming down with something. I don't know."

"Really?" Lela asked with concern. "Your face is red. Do you have a fever?"

"No, I'm fine. Honest. It just seems warm in here for some reason."

"Kay, I understand that you've been staying at Lela's house. That was a very kind thing for Lela to do. Saving you from the inside of a hotel room for weeks on end."

Kay snapped the edge of the plastic menu with her thumb, eyes studying Grace over the top of the left page just above the list of appetizers. "I'm grateful to Lela for her hospitality. While I don't mind traveling, staying in a hotel room is not one of my favorite things to do."

"It was really not a problem for Kay to stay with me. I have plenty of room, and I have enjoyed the company. Unfortunately, I have been living alone for a long time."

The waiter interrupted again and scribbled down their orders. Grace also requested a bottle of champagne. "It may be premature to celebrate, but I think tomorrow's meeting will prove to be successful for all of us."

"No doubt," Kay agreed. "From what you outlined to us earlier over the phone, I think the fact that the government has exposed a large environmental sabotage effort will communicate to Alaskans that their interests are being properly guarded."

Lela shook her head. "I cannot believe what these people planned to do. Poison the land with this terrible chemical. I know this much — all of this has distracted my attention away from the National Petroleum Reserve. Oil spills are damaging, but we can deal with those. We have in the past. My people have in the past. But benzene in the water — that is another matter entirely."

"The larger effort to stop the terrorists will not deter me from the smaller effort to keep the oil companies in line," Grace said emphatically. "No matter what public relations spin we put on all of this, the fact of the matter is that so far the oil companies have been compliant with the lease agreements in the reserve. We are investigating that one infraction, the buildings you two found. But other than that the oil companies have come up clean. Quite frankly, that surprises me. I shouldn't say this, but when the complaints started flooding in from environmental groups and the Northern Council, I saw my career dissolving before my eyes."

"I think that comes from that fact that in the past the oil companies have been less than cooperative." Kay accepted her platter from the waiter. "But the Exxon *Valdez* accident changed all that forever. The Alaskan people will never forget, and the government now knows that restrictions have to be enforced and complaints investigated."

Grace nodded in agreement. "You are so right. What are you eating there, Kay?"

"Some kind of fish. I don't know. But it's good."

Lela laughed. "It is the grayling you would not order when you were here last."

"Here last?" Grace asked.

"Yes, I brought Kay here for lunch when she first arrived. Then she ordered the whitefish."

"I'm not very brave."

Grace looked at Lela, then back at Kay. "Oh, I think you're brave, Miss Westmore. In fact, I think we should toast to that."

The three women touched glasses, and Kay took a healthy swallow. "Thanks, Grace. Thanks for the dinner."

"You're welcome. I appreciate all the good work you've both done. Lela, do you think the Northern Council will be receptive to our findings tomorrow?"

"Yes, I do. The information we present will tell my people that the government is protecting the land. That the history of the Exxon disaster will not repeat itself inland. That the Teshekpuk Lake region is safe for the wildlife and the people."

Grace tapped her fingers impatiently against the table. "When you refer to 'my people,' what exactly do you mean?"

"They are my people in heritage, in race."

"Well, they're my people, too," Grace said. "They're my people to serve, and they're Americans just like me. Furthermore, the land is just as important to me as it is to them."

"I don't think anyone questions your dedication, Secretary Perry." Lela fiddled with her napkin, twisting it around her finger. "Or your motives. I do not pretend to know everything you hear in Washington. All I can tell you is that the Inupiat and other native tribes are trying to live as they have always lived. But it is hard. I do not think they see the government as an enemy. The elders do not always understand because they know only the old ways. The young understand full well that the world outside their village progresses. Some join that world more fully than others do. But all want to preserve their culture and identity. Without it we fade away. I think you will understand this better tomorrow."

191

"I think I understand it better now because you've done such an eloquent job of explaining it to me. Forgive me if I sounded rude. They are your people and I respect that. You know them far better than I ever will. I'm assuming that Kay has learned all this from you as well."

"I have," Kay answered. "Lela speaks well for her people and for the government."

Grace refilled their glasses. "That's why she's such a good lawyer. She can argue both cases and be just as convincing on one side as the other."

Straight-faced Lela said, "*Good lawyer* is an oxymoron, is it not?"

"Just like *good government*," Kay said, laughing.

Grace frowned. "Miss Westmore, I expect a little more loyalty out of you. Even if what you say is true."

Thursday morning the weather cooperated. The sky was a pristine blue without a storm cloud for miles. This time the meeting with the Inupiat Northern Council and other local community groups was held at a downtown Barrow hotel. The meeting room was larger and more suitable for the number of people expected. Kay watched the crowd file in, at least four hundred people or more — and once again it was standing room only. The press was out in full force, taking up the first three rows of chairs. Bulbs flashed as television camera personnel and local news anchors tested their equipment.

Meanwhile, Grace stood calmly near the front podium as the technicians ran wires and tested audiovisual equipment. Grace's staff in Washington had prepared quite a show — complete with computerized slides, graphs, maps, and other electronic wizardry. Kay was to do the initial introductions and then take a seat for the rest of the proceedings. When she spied Stone Allen sitting midway down the fifth row of chairs, she was happy for the small role.

"Our job is a little easier today. Grace will do the hard work," Lela said, sitting down at the dais next to Kay.

"Not long ago, I was to be the star of this event."

Kay shook her head. "That's Grace. She's always stealing the show."

"From this vantage point, I am glad."

"So am I."

About ten minutes later, Kay made Grace's introduction. She spoke briefly about Grace's tenure as the director and then secretary of the interior. "Secretary Perry has a great deal of information to share with you today concerning the Teshekpuk Lake investigation and some other land issues we know will be of great interest to you."

Kay sat down, and Grace began with a review of the Teshekpuk Lake investigation and the findings concerning the areas not leased to the oil companies for exploration. She underscored the government's commitment to protecting the areas that were off limits — and the fact that these areas were found to be free from any violations by the oil companies. There was a murmur of disbelief in the audience, but Grace continued undaunted. "There was one oil company work area found inside the protected zone. As a result, the Alyeska Consortium will be fined three million dollars."

At this announcement, the crowd sat in stunned silence. It was a heavy fine for two abandoned buildings and a couple of rogue drill beds. Kay glanced at Stone Allen. His face turned a deep shade of red. After the news of the stiff penalty against the oil companies had finally sunk in, the crowd started to come alive with cheers and applause.

Then Grace began her multimedia presentation that centered on the benzene found in eight different locations throughout the National Petroleum Reserve including the Teshekpuk Lake area. Again, the room was deathly quiet. "The environmental terrorists were caught three days ago in Idaho. The benzene was tracked to a manufacturing source in Japan. The chemical was sold legally into the United States but was reported stolen from the buyer in October. EPA was notified, and that's how Interior got involved. We've been tracking the chemical, fearing this kind of terrorism ever since."

Grace continued with slides showing what the benzene would do to the ground water and surrounding land if released. "The consequences would be devastating. Benzene is one of the most lethal chemicals in existence. There's no way to clean this stuff up, my friends. If the fumes don't kill you first, it seeps into the ground, contaminates the water, and keeps running through the earth like a thunderbolt. The chemical would be transported through water, contaminating rivers and streams. It would also contaminate underground water. Animals would drink the water and die. People would become ill and die more slowly. Benzene is a known carcinogen."

Shutting down the computer, Grace paced in front of the room. "My message to all of you is that the government will continue to be vigilant, whether it's to police the oil companies, if need be, or to investigate and prevent environmental terrorism. Sometimes we think the enemy is one we know, one we can identify because they seem to live in our own backyard. But I'm here to tell you that many times the worst enemy is the one we cannot see. That enemy is by far the most dangerous and deadly."

Lela called the meeting to a close, giving the Northern Council representatives and locals the opportunity to ask questions. To Kay's utter surprise, there were none. Instead, all the people lined up in front of the room to shake Grace's hand, then Lela's and her own. The line snaked from the lip of the stage to the front door. People waited patiently for an hour for the brief opportunity to thank them for protecting their homes, their small villages, their way of life. Grace basked in the moment, and Kay saw that Grace had been right. The truth was the best public relations there was.

After the meeting concluded, Stone Allen insisted on

taking a final opportunity to infuriate Kay. He interrupted her in the middle of a conversation by tapping her on the shoulder. Kay swung around to find his smirking face. "What do you want?"

"Just to tell you what an immense pleasure it was working with you."

"Oh, please."

"No, really. It was gratifying to witness firsthand your inability to hang the oil companies out to dry again, which was your intention, of course."

"That was never my intention, and you know it."

"Now who will you and your environmentalist friends target?"

"I have no doubt that there will be other investigations involving the oil companies. Sooner or later, your consortium will do something stupid again. Like foul up half of Alaska with another oil slick. Although I really wish you wouldn't. You've killed and maimed enough wildlife for a lifetime, haven't you?"

"The oil company consortium represents the future of this country. Generation Y won't even remember Prince William Sound or the part Exxon played. Meanwhile, they'll all be driving gas-guzzling SUVs," Allen growled. "And bleeding-heart organizations like the National Wildlife Federation will be bankrupt."

"Allen, don't you have somewhere to go? Some press releases to draft? A check to write for a three-million-dollar fine?"

"That was just a slap on the wrist."

"It won't be the last."

Allen's remarks set the tone for the rest of the afternoon. While Lela and Grace met with representatives from the Inupiat Northern Council, Kay retreated to a smaller meeting room the government had rented for the day. She set up her laptop and was completing her final reports on the recent investigation when Grace Perry walked into the room.

Grace rummaged through her briefcase and then glanced over at Kay. "How do you think it went, Kay?"

"Seemed to go fine," Kay mumbled, eyes skimming the paragraph she had just completed.

"Lela's still meeting with the council. They seem quite impressed with what they heard today."

"That's good."

"You don't seem impressed."

"Was there ever any doubt about the outcome?"

"Miss Westmore, what's wrong with you?"

Kay peered over the top of the screen. "Nothing."

"Yes, well you've been behaving oddly since I arrived. I'm only wondering when you're going to talk about it."

"Is this still a professional conversation, Grace? Or has it turned personal now?"

Grace slapped some files down on the table. "We can make this conversation whatever you'd like it to be. Or we can make it nothing at all."

Looking almost hurt, Grace began fiddling with her Palm Pilot. "Have you figured that thing out yet?"

"Of course not."

"I'm sorry, Grace. Allen put me in a bad mood. He's such a pompous idiot."

"Ass."

"That, too."

"I've sent him back to the consortium and all his equally pompous higher-ups. I'm sorry you had to put up with him."

"I've put up with worse."

Grace made another face at her Palm Pilot. "I will learn to work this thing, I swear." Grace smiled and slipped the small computer back into its leather case. "Seems like you and Lela hit it off well."

Kay's fingers continued to run smoothly over the

computer keys, but her palms were sweating. "Working with Lela was terrific," Kay mumbled while typing. "She and I and Russ made a great team. The team members from EPA were also first-rate."

"I'm glad to hear that. And now you'll go back to Fairbanks and all the paperwork."

"Yes. That's true."

Grace pulled up a chair. "Kay, I'm thinking about consolidating some offices in Fairbanks. The EPA office is in Anchorage, and the Bureau of Land Management has several offices and employees at various locations. Consolidation in Fairbanks will save the government a lot of money. Plus it would give you the administrative support you need to dig out from underneath the paperwork. What do you think of that idea?"

Kay stopped typing. Now Grace had her undivided attention. "Sounds wonderful. I could get out into the field more. Do what I do best again. Be more of a support to you in Washington."

"Needless to say, I won't be secretary of the interior forever, so we'll need to do this reorganization within the next six months. Take a look at this plan I've drafted. Make some notes and send it to me after you get back to Fairbanks."

"I'll give it my complete attention."

"Good. When will you be leaving?"

"For home?"

"Yes."

"I suppose Monday's soon enough. I might as well stay out the weekend. I've made some friends here. Need to say good-bye to a few people."

"Lela?"

"Her most of all."

"I thought so."

"It was probably written all over our faces."

"Actually, it was. Besides, I've always been able to read you like a book."

"You read everyone like a book."

"Listen, Russ can take care of things for a few more days. You don't have to rush back." Grace zipped her briefcase. "I, on the other hand, must get back. The government can't operate without me at the helm, you know."

"You sound like Alexander Haig." Kay puffed up her chest. "I'm in charge here."

Opening the door, Grace laughed. "You'd be surprised. Take care, Kay."

Kay finished slicing cheese and then opened the wine. A dry Chardonnay with a snappy bouquet, the bottle had cost her thirty dollars. In the lower forty-eight states, the same bottle retailed at thirteen dollars. But Kay had grown accustomed to the high cost of living in Alaska, and the government pay she earned reflected that reality. Others were not so fortunate. In Barrow, alcohol was frequently purchased on the black market for even higher prices. Shortages and low wages made a bottle of wine a luxury.

"Is it a good wine?"

Kay had just taken her first sip. "Very good. It should be for what I paid."

"For most people in Barrow, there is no such thing as a bad bottle of wine. If there is a bottle of wine it is enough."

"In Fairbanks supply shortages are not usually a problem, but the prices are just as bad." Kay handed Lela a glass. "For you, I would walk ten miles and pay a hundred dollars."

"Thank you, Kay."

"A toast to you, my love."

"And to you. And a safe trip tomorrow."

"That brings up the question, when will I see you again?"

"I can visit Fairbanks in a couple of weeks."

"And what happens after that? Another couple of weeks

goes by. I visit Barrow, you visit Fairbanks?" Kay forced a laugh. "We won't go broke on wine. We'll go broke on airfare."

"Then maybe it cannot be so often."

"We need to talk about this, Lela. The distance will kill our relationship, and I don't want to lose you."

"But what can we do? It is reality and we knew this from the beginning."

"You can move to Fairbanks. Work out of the government office there."

"I am sure Grace Perry will have something to say about that."

"She already has." Kay reached over Lela to the dinette table and snatched the file folders she had been reviewing. "Grace has plans to centralize state offices in Fairbanks. This includes some employees, like yourself, who are working in satellite regions."

Lela stared at the folders. "Yes, I must confess. I have known about this. Grace mentioned it to me a few days ago."

"Why didn't you say something?"

"Because I did not know what to say or do."

"So you pretended not to know?"

"Yes. It was an unkind thing to do."

"Lela, it means we can be together."

"Barrow is my home. It has been my home for all of my life. How can I leave now?"

"You can leave for us."

"My people are here."

"Your people hardly know you. They know you as a government lawyer — and you would still be doing that work in Fairbanks. You would still be helping your people, Lela. That's not going to change."

"I want to be with you, Kay, but I am not sure I can leave my home."

"Then you obviously don't love me enough." Kay started to pace. The room became a blur. Her mind raced with angry thoughts. "I'd hoped that what we had was different, but I don't know why. It's always the same. Every relationship is the same, and none of them last. There's no commitment, no desire to overcome the smallest obstacles. It's too easy to just move on to someone else. Why? Why is it so hard to love that way? Completely and honestly."

"Kay, you are not making any sense. I do love you. That is not the issue."

"The only issue for you is Barrow? Is that what you're telling me?"

"Yes."

"I don't believe you."

"I cannot change your thoughts. There is an old native saying. Think what you want to think. You have to live with your thoughts."

Kay suddenly lost the fight to control her temper. "If I could persuade Grace Perry and the United States government to move the entire Alaskan Interior Department to Barrow, I'd do it in a heartbeat. I would move here for you, Lela. There would be no question."

"That is easy for you to analogize. You do not have to move or leave your people or the land that holds the spirits of your ancestors. I know no other place. It is not just about love. It is who I will be if I move. You are thinking only of yourself."

"That's not true at all. I'm thinking about us and what we have. I'm not thinking about anything else."

"What we have will survive if it is strong."

"And that's easy for you to say. I've been through this kind of thing before, and I don't know if I can be strong anymore. I don't know if I can take another risk or if I even want to. I've lost too much already in disastrous relationships, and I don't want to lose any more. I'd rather give you up now than go on hoping that this thing can work with us living hundreds of miles apart. Why bother when I know already that it can't work?"

"You seem to have all the answers."

"You haven't offered any. You're just sitting there. You're not even angry."

"You are angry enough for both of us."

"Maybe I can't take any more."

"Are you saying good-bye, Kay?"

"I guess so. I'll go to the hotel tonight and leave tomorrow."

"We still have time to talk."

"There's nothing more to say. We all do what we have to do. You have to stay. I have to go."

Chapter Twelve

The plane ride back to Fairbanks on Friday was agonizing. Kay sat for hours with her eyes closed, reliving every moment with Lela. She couldn't believe it was over. Her body and mind were numb with regret. Getting off the plane, she didn't even go home. She headed straight for Alex and Pat's house.

Alex greeted her with a hug and kiss. And then Kay broke down. Alex held her for an hour until Pat came home. Pat encouraged Kay to get some rest. "Take a nap before dinner. You look beat, hon."

Kay slept for a couple of hours. When she woke up she staggered out of the guest room into the den. Pat was hunched over the computer.

"What're you doing there, buddy?"

Pat flashed a satisfied grin. "Killing off the nasties of the world. It's a hoot."

"How's it work?"

"Aw, hell, it's easy. See, if you hit the left mouse button you can kill all these bad guys. The right button reloads your weapon." Pat slid the mouse back and forth across the mouse pad, leaving a pile of terrorist bodies lying bloodied in the streets. "It's a great way to relieve stress."

Kay put her hand on Pat's shoulder. "If only I had taken this game with me to Anakruak. Lord knows I had enough stress to relieve while I was there."

"Sounds like you found a way to relieve it." Pat winked, her brown eyes filled with mischief. "A much more fun way."

"I'm going upstairs to find your wife. Something smells good, and I want to know what she's cooking."

Pat got up and poured Kay a glass of wine from the downstairs bar. "She won't let me in the kitchen."

"Like you're dying to get in there and help."

"No, of course not. My job's to keep the property in shape. You know, all the manly chores."

"Yeah, so I heard. How's the garage?"

"Still a little charred. Nothing some paint won't fix."

"Well, I know who to call when I need something soldered."

"Damn. Al's ruining my butch reputation."

"Nah, I think it's safe."

Kay wandered through the house, following the aroma of spices and onions. She stopped in the living room to stare at a new painting and sip her wine. It was a watercolor of running horses, their heads tossed back with full manes blowing in the wind. It reminded her of Lela — her strong but gentle spirit moving through a room unharnessed and free, controlled by no one. How could Kay expect to tame such a spirit? To redirect that spirit against her will? It had been a foolish thing to hope and a selfish thing to ask.

Kay poked her head into the kitchen. Alex was stir-frying

a large pan of vegetables. The steam rose around her face and enveloped the dark hair that fell in curls across her shoulders. "Smells good. Am I allowed in?"

"You are. Where's Pat?"

"Not to worry. She's downstairs making the world safe from terrorists."

"Isn't that your job?"

"Not any more. I gladly relinquish it."

Alex stopped stirring and kissed Kay lightly on the cheek. "You look like hell."

"Thanks. That's exactly how I feel."

"Have you spoken to Lela since you got back to Fairbanks?"

"No, I came right over here. I doubt she'll speak to me, and I don't really blame her. I blew it, Al. Making demands like that. I don't know what I was thinking."

"You're in love, honey. No one thinks when they're in love."

"You're my best friend. Can I ask you a question?"

"Of course, Kay."

"Do you think I'm insecure?"

Alex stood next to Kay and put her arm around Kay's shoulder. "Well, sometimes you talk tough, but I think maybe you're not that tough on the inside." Squeezing Kay's shoulder, Alex said, "Everyone's afraid, Kay. Some of us can admit that and talk about it. You find it hard."

"You know me too well."

"What are you afraid of?"

"Everything. Every damned thing."

Pat strode into the kitchen and grabbed a beer from the refrigerator. "Go back to Barrow, grab Lela by the hair, and put her on a plane. That's my advice."

Kay started to laugh, but Alex shot Pat a look of horror. "Pat! This is no time for jokes."

204

Pointing at Kay with her beer bottle, Pat said, "Look at her. The woman's dying. She could use some laughs."

"It's okay, Al. She's right. Laughter's a good thing."

Pat sat down and stretched out her long legs. She ran her hand through her short, blond hair and shook her head. "I haven't met Lela, of course. But, listen, if she's been married and is a bit of a femme from what I can gather, you gotta be the strong one. Be the decision-maker. Soft women like that."

Kay laughed until her sides hurt.

"What's so damned funny?" Pat asked.

"It's a good thing you missed the conversation Al and I just had. Otherwise, you'd know just how funny that sounded."

"Pat, you're insane." Alex tossed some chicken in with the vegetables. "Lela's lived alone in the wilderness for the past seven years. I would hardly call that soft."

Pat swigged her beer. "Yeah, you got a point there."

"She's a completely free spirit," Kay said, leaning against the refrigerator. "Lela's like the wind. You can feel her all around, but you can't hold her against her will. Barrow has been her home for her entire life. I'm not sure I could leave either. She has a connection with the people and the land there. It's a spiritual thing, something only the Inupiat understand. I was being pompous to dismiss it like it was nothing at all. Like I was somehow more important than a lifetime of family and personal history."

"Okay, so you lost it. So you got a little short-tempered." Pat leaned back in her chair. "Could have happened to anyone."

"It happened to me because I've got a problem with my temper. I've got a problem facing things. So I end up acting badly. I had a lot of time to think on the plane."

Alex reached for Kay's empty wineglass. "Kay, if she really loves you, your short fuse isn't what matters. Or your fears.

205

If all you say about Lela is true, it's her connection to the land and her people that she's struggling with. Maybe she has some fears of her own."

The weekend passed in a blur. Kay stayed at Alex and Pat's house until Sunday afternoon when she finally went home to her own apartment. Emotionally exhausted, she showered Sunday evening and went to bed. When the alarm woke her up for work Monday morning, she couldn't believe she had slept for over twelve hours. All she could remember from that night of long sleep were some strange dreams about Lela. Lela herding caribou across the open tundra. Lela sewing animal hides in a circle with other Inupiat women. Lela chanting prayers in her native language and cleaning a rifle for the summer caribou hunt. In the dream, all their moments together had ceased to exist. Lela had gone back to her people, was no longer a government attorney, and had even married Thaddeus. Kay had tried to fight the dreams off, but each dream had run into the next until she woke to the buzzing of the alarm clock.

It was still early when she arrived at the office, about six-thirty. She was the first one there. Shutting her office door, she stayed hidden away, hoping to remain incognito for as long as possible. But eventually someone noticed her car in the parking lot and then there was a knock at the door. It was Rachel, which was no surprise.

"Kay, what are you doing here? I thought you weren't due back until later today."

"I caught an earlier flight." Kay didn't even look up from her quarterly budget report. "So what's been happening around here?"

"Not much. Russ has been working all hours. But I do have some things for you to sign. Everything's in your signature folder."

"Thanks."

"Are you okay?"

Kay made eye contact. It could no longer be avoided. "I'm fine," she lied. "Just tired."

One eyebrow arched above the other, Rachel grabbed Kay's empty coffee cup. "Oh, okay. I'll get you some more coffee."

"That's not necessary."

"No problem. Really."

"Thanks."

When Rachel returned with her coffee, Russ was tagging along right behind. "Hey, I heard you were in. Couldn't wait to get back to the old grind, eh?"

"No, I couldn't stand to be away for another second."

"Look at her," Rachel said with a note of sarcasm. "She's so happy to be back, can't you tell?"

"Rachel, can you put a call through to Grace Perry and let her know that I have returned to the office and just how happy I am?" Kay smiled and sipped her coffee. "And thank you for the coffee."

"Sure. I'll go call Grace right away."

Russ shut the door. For a minute he just stood there staring at her.

"Are you going to stand there and stare too?"

"Okay, what did Grace do now? She sending us on another benzene run or what?"

"No. Everything's back to normal. Say, did I tell you about the reorg Grace is planning? Consolidating some of the satellite offices here in Fairbanks?"

"You faxed me a copy of the memo on Thursday."

"Oh, I couldn't remember. Anyway, what do you think?"

"I think it'll save a lot of money and should have been done a long time ago." Russ studied Kay intently. "I also think you look like hell and I'm wonderin' what's goin' on."

"I look like hell? Why thank you, Russ. That's so sweet of you to say."

"Listen, I've known you long enough to be able to figure out when somethin's up. Big time."

"It's personal, Russ."

"Yeah, so you can't tell me personal stuff now? We're not friends anymore?"

"Of course we are. It's just that the whole thing's a mess and was totally inappropriate to begin with, which is probably why I'm feeling like shit right now — because I deserve to feel this way."

"Somehow, I kinda doubt that."

"Okay. Lela and I became very close during our trip. Now we're not close anymore. I fucked things up real good. It's all my fault, really."

"Can't you two kiss and make up?"

"Russell."

"I'm not bein' funny. My wife and I do it all the time. It's part of bein' married, you know. I fuck up, she fucks up. I have a bad day, she has a bad day. It happens to people. The question is, what're you gonna do about it?"

"The relationship wasn't exactly appropriate workwise. That could be a problem, too."

"Why? Lela don't report to you. She reports to Bill Sadler, the director of the Bureau of Land Management in D.C. He reports to Perry. I don't see a problem there."

"I'm overreacting, aren't I?"

"Yeah, you are. Listen, I don't know what happened between you two, and it ain't none of my business. But you need to grab it by the tail and deal with it, Kay. Don't let it eat you up like this. You know, like the Stef thing. You can't make that right 'cause she left you. But maybe you can make this thing with Lela right and finally be happy. I think Lela's a hell of a person."

"Well, you're just full of opinions."

"That ain't what I'm full of, but you asked."

"Yes, I did. Thanks, Russ."

"For what?"

"For being a friend. Alex and Pat were friends all weekend. They'll probably never let me back in their house again. Now you. You're all terrific and I'm very lucky."

"Don't mention it. Say, I approved about a billion dollars worth of expenses while you were gone. Hope you don't mind."

"Not at all. Did you refurbish the entire building?"

"Just about."

"Get me a government car?"

"It's on order."

"Good. Then our budget's shot for the rest of the year and I don't have to sign any more damned forms."

Russ laughed and got up. "I'll let you get some work done. Hang in there."

Kay's hand rested on the phone while she fingered the plastic calling card. It was time to make a decision and live with it. It was time to call Lela.

Lela answered the phone, and Kay summoned all the courage she had. "Lela, it's Kay."

Lela's voice was devoid of emotion. "Hello, Kay."

"I wanted to call you and apologize for my behavior. I had no right to demand things of you. No right to have such unreasonable expectations. I've done a lot of thinking and I've faced a lot of demons since I saw you last." Kay's palms were sweating, and a surge of fear washed over her. She closed her eyes and swallowed hard, determined to accept whatever was to come. "Sooner or later I've got to learn to live with my insecurities and my rash judgments. I really didn't give you a chance to say what you needed to say when we spoke last because I was afraid to hear it. But I'd like to give you that chance now. Or at least the chance to tell me to go to hell. Your choice."

There was silence on the other end of the line. Kay could

hear Lela breathing, and she steadied herself mentally for whatever Lela had to say.

"I do not know what to say to you, Kay. I have been thinking a lot too. But I have not decided anything."

"I understand. Take as much time as you need."

"I will. Thank you for calling."

Kay hung up the phone and fought for composure. She wondered if she had learned from her mistakes in time.

By the third glass of wine, Kay was beginning to feel pleasantly numb. Twice that evening she had almost called Lela again but had stopped herself at the last moment. The knock at the door forced a deep growl from her throat. She was in no mood for company or solicitations. Wearily, she stumbled toward the door and opened it. She blinked a few times before the image of Stef imprinted itself on her wine-besotted brain.

"Stef?"

"Hi ya, Kay. Mind if I come in for a few minutes?"

"No. Not at all." Kay closed the door and plopped down on the sofa. "I'm sorry. I should take your coat."

Stef threw her coat over the recliner. "That's okay. Don't get up again."

"You want a glass of wine?" Kay picked up the bottle and peered inside it. "I think there's enough for one more glass."

Stef grinned sweetly. "No. I can't stay long. I was just wondering if you'd had time to think about our last conversation. I never heard from you, Kay. I think I know what that means, but I couldn't stand not really knowing. So here I am. If I'm being a big pain, just tell me and I'll go."

"You don't have to go. Not at all. And you're not a big pain."

"Good. How are you, Kay?"

"I'm just peachy. Couldn't be better. And you?"

"Well, things aren't any better with Jan. In fact, we've pretty much packed it in. Like, I just couldn't deal with it any more. Plus I told her I was still in love with you and that I'd made a terrible mistake."

Kay squinted hard. "You told her that?"

"Yeah."

"Gosh. That must have made an impression. Stef, you know, you really need to learn some diplomacy or something." Kay chuckled. "Listen to me. I'm the queen of diplomacy. Oh brother."

"Well, I don't know much about diplomacy. I thought being totally honest was best. You kinda have to be blunt with Jan."

The word *honest* was immediately sobering to Kay. "Honest. Yes, that's what I should've been the last time we spoke."

"Weren't you?"

"Not to the extent that I should've been. I mean, I needed to tell you some things and I didn't."

"Why, Kay?"

"Because I'm a damned coward. But I'm going to correct that mistake now." Kay drained the wineglass and set the empty glass on the coffee table. "This is a hard thing for me to say, but it's over between us, Stef. Permanently over." Stef started to speak, but Kay held up her hand. "Please. Let me finish. There are a couple of reasons it's over. One, because I screwed up. I started taking our relationship for granted, taking you for granted.

"Two, because I worked hard to let you go, and it was hell. I don't know how else to describe it. Whatever I looked like on the outside, on the inside I was dying. But somehow I got through it all by convincing myself that all I wanted was for you to be happy. It was a bullshit lie I told myself because I didn't have the guts to face the truth."

Kay stared at the empty wineglass again and then poured the last of the wine for herself. At that particular moment in time, she really didn't care about being polite.

"Third reason is that I've met someone else." Stef let out an audible gasp, but Kay kept right on talking. "Her name's Lela Newlin, and I met in her in Barrow two months ago. I don't know how just yet, but she's the woman I'm going to spend the rest of my life with." Taking a sip of wine, Kay peered at Stef over the top of her glass. Stef's face was streaming with tears, and Kay started to cry too. "I'm sorry, Stef. I really am."

Stef closed her eyes and shook her head as if to wake herself from a bad dream. "I guess I've just made a total ass out of myself. This week has ended on an even crappier note than it started. Like, if I had known this was going to be the shittiest week of my life, I'd've written it all down in some freakin' journal. What not to do the next time I get it in my mind to try to make things right with everyone."

"Is that what you were trying to do? Make things right with me?"

"Yes."

"Making things right and loving me are two entirely different matters, Stef. The one doesn't necessarily fix the other. It doesn't fix the mistakes I made either."

"I don't care what you're saying right now. You're . . . like twisting my words or something. I love you, Kay. That's it."

"That should've been it because I loved you, too. If I'd worked hard enough to show it all along, things would've been different. I didn't, and that's why you left. But if it's any consolation at all, you taught me something, Stef. Enough for me to be able to say that I don't plan on making the same mistakes this time around."

The next evening after work, Kay stopped by to see her father. She hadn't visited with him since she had returned from Barrow, and she was anxious to spend some time with him. When she got to his room she found out he was in whirlpool therapy, so she sat down on the sofa and thumbed through a magazine. She had slipped deep into a paralyzing funk again since her unexpected visit from Stef last night. After Stef left, she had tried to call Lela, but there had been no answer. She waited another hour and called again. Still no answer. Where was she, Kay wondered. Where was Lela?

"Kay, they're bringing Daddy down the hall now."

Glancing up, Kay noticed Julia walking in the door. She was dressed in a tight knit dress that flattered her curvaceous figure. She was stunning — and suddenly different, though Kay couldn't quite understand why. "How is Pop?"

"Getting better every day."

"Good."

"How are you, Kay? You look . . . tired or something."

Kay smiled. "I like your dress."

"What did you say?"

"I said, I like your dress. It's really hot."

Julia's mouth dropped almost to her cleavage. "Why thank you, Kay. How sweet."

"Here he is," Kay said. The attendant brought their father in and helped him into his motorized recliner.

"Daddy, look. Kay's here. She's back from Barrow."

"Kay. Glad you're back."

Kay hugged her father. "Glad to be home, Pop. How are you feeling?"

"Better. I like the whirlpool."

Julia sat down next to her dad and held his hand. "Are you home for good now, Kay?"

"I think so. I mean, I don't have any trips planned for the immediate future." Kay swallowed hard. She had hoped to plan some trips to see Lela in Barrow. That was unlikely now. "But you never know what this job has in store."

"Are you going to get your old job back?" her father asked, tilting his head to the side. "You liked it better."

"I don't think so, Pop. I may get to travel more, but the backside of a desk seems to be in my future."

"Too bad."

"It's okay. I'm actually getting used to it."

"Kay, Jack's out of town on business, so I'm going to have Daddy over for dinner all this week. I thought he might enjoy that."

"I'm sure he's thrilled. Aren't you, Pop?"

"Julie's a great cook."

"Yes, she is. Say, Julia, do you think I could join you one night? For dinner?"

Julia looked at Kay like she was an alien suddenly dropped from the sky. "You want to come over to dinner? To my house for dinner?"

"I'll bring the wine," Kay offered, smiling.

"That would be wonderful, Kay. Won't it, Daddy?"

"Yes, I'd like that."

"Kay, come over tomorrow. I'll make Mom's chicken recipe. You know, the one you like so much with the broccoli and cheese."

"Chicken divan."

"That's it."

"Fantastic. Hey, Pop. You want me to bring dessert, too? Some ice cream?"

Her father smiled. "Vanilla."

Tuesday evening, after dinner with her sister and father, Kay opened the door to her apartment. Turning on the light in the foyer, she threw her keys in a bowl on the small oak table that had been her mother's. She turned around and caught the outline of a shadow on the living room sofa.

"Your apartment is just like you, Kay. Precise, tasteful, simple. Everything has a place."

"Lela?"

"Russ let me in with his emergency key. Apparently, you used to have a cat his wife fed from time to time."

"Moose."

Lela laughed. "You had a cat named Moose?"

"Yes. He died about a year ago."

"You did not tell me you were an animal lover. There is so much more to learn about you."

"Other than the fact that I have a bad temper."

"You have a temper. But I would not call it bad."

"I tried to call you last night." Kay's face flushed. "I shouldn't have but I did."

"And you did not get me because I was on my way here."

"I just had dinner with Julia and Pop."

"Really? How did it go?"

"We had a lot of fun, actually. My sister and I may not always see eye to eye but we're headed down a much better road. That makes me very happy."

"That is wonderful, Kay."

"We can make this work, Lela. I was wrong."

"So was I. There comes a time in life when new places and new people are needed. Earlier, when I found that you were not here, I walked down to the river and looked across to the mountains above Fairbanks."

"And what did you see?"

"My life here with you."

Kay hid her face in her hands and cried the tears she had been fighting for days. Then she felt Lela's arms around her waist.

"Do not hide your tears, Kay. If they are tears of joy, then I want to see them, too."

Kay uncovered her face and Lela reached up, wiping a tear from her cheek. "I thought the nights seemed like forever with you in my arms, Lela. But they were a hell of a lot longer without you."

"The days and nights are both long without you, my darling. *Nakuaqqun*, Kay. *Nakuaqqun*."

"I hope that means what I think it means."

"This is what it means." Lela put her arms around Kay's

215

neck and kissed her deeply. "Love. For the last time I have found it."

"And I for the first time."

Kay reached over to the wall switch and turned off the light. When she had first met Lela it had been night, a long, cold Alaskan night that hung over the snow and the pine forests like an impenetrable dark curtain. Now, in the darkness of the room, Kay held the softness of Lela close as the night found them together once again.

```
WI041 IMPORTANT! CHOICE PRIVILEGES ARRIVALS & STAYOV
------------------------------------------------------
Choice Privileges program members who will arrive o
property today are listed below.  Please remember t
any local reservation and walk-in members, with the

    * express check-in                 * complimentar
    * free local calls                  * free incomi
    * complimentary USA TODAY           * late checko


------------------------------------------------------
Arrival    Nts Conf #   Guest Name             Mem
------------------------------------------------------
05/04/2002  3  31701355 PAUL PLUEMER            PC
05/05/2002  1  33315890 LEIGH HANSON            LC
---- End of List ----

See Redemption Voucher for more information on C

REMEMBER - Choice Privileges Worldwide members d
will not appear on your TAI and you will not be
Thus, any Choice Privileges Worldwide local res
not be added to your TAI.




TRAN:05MAY/0237    DLVR:05May/0444    MSGNBR:12
```

About the Author

Laura DeHart Young is a native Pennsylvanian. She has written five romance novels: *There Will Be No Goodbyes, Family Secrets, Love on the Line, Private Passions,* and *Intimate Stranger. Forever and the Night* is her sixth book and her first published by Bella Books. When not writing for Bella Books, Laura works as a communications director for an information technology company. Her career took her to beautiful Atlanta, Georgia, where she now lives with her beloved pug, Dudley.

Publications from
BELLA BOOKS, INC.
The best in contemporary lesbian fiction

P.O. Box 201007   Ferndale, MI 48220
Phone: 800-729-4992
www.bellabooks.com

FOREVER AND THE NIGHT by Laura DeHart Young. 224 pp.
Desire and passion ignite the frozen Arctic in this exciting sequel
to the classic romantic adventure   *Love on the Line.*
                                ISBN 0-931513-00-7 $11.95

WINGED ISIS by Jean Stewart. 240 pp. The long-awaited sequel
to *Warriors of Isis* and the fourth in the exciting Isis series.
                                ISBN 1-931513-01-5 $11.95

ROOM FOR LOVE by Frankie J. Jones. 192 pp. Jo and Beth must
overcome the past in order to have a future together.
                                ISBN 0-9677753-9-6 $11.95

THE QUESTION OF SABOTAGE by Bonnie J. Morris. 144 pp. A
charming, sexy tale of romance, intrigue, and coming of age.
                                ISBN 0-9677753-8-8 $11.95

SLEIGHT OF HAND by Karin Kallmaker writing as Laura Adams.
256 pp. A journey of passion, heartbreak and triumph that reunites
two women for a final chance at their destiny. ISBN 0-9677753-7-X $11.95

MOVING TARGETS: A Helen Black Mystery by Pat Welch.
240 pp. Helen must decide if getting to the bottom of a mystery
is worth hitting bottom.   ISBN 0-9677753-6-1 $11.95

CALM BEFORE THE STORM by Peggy J. Herring. 208 pp. Colonel
Robicheaux retires from the military and comes out of the closet.
                                ISBN 0-9677753-1-0 $11.95

OFF SEASON by Jackie Calhoun. 208 pp. Pam threatens Jenny
and Rita's fledgling relationship.   ISBN 0-9677753-0-2 $11.95

WHEN EVIL CHANGES FACE: A Motor City Thriller by Therese
Szymanski. 240 pp. Brett Higgins is back in another heart-pounding
thriller.   ISBN 0-9677753-3-7 $11.95

BOLD COAST LOVE by Diana Tremain Braund. 208 pp. Jackie
Claymont fights for her reputation and the right to love the woman
she chooses.   ISBN 0-9677753-2-9 $11.95

THE WILD ONE by Lyn Denison. 176 pp. Rachel never expected that Quinn's wild yearnings would change her life forever.
ISBN 0-9677753-4-5 $11.95

SWEET FIRE by Saxon Bennett. 224 pp. Welcome to Heroy — the town with the most lesbians per capita than any other place on the planet!
ISBN 0-9677753-5-3 $11.95

Visit
Bella Books
at

www.bellabooks.com